PARADISE
CLOSE

ALSO BY LISA RUSS SPAAR

POETRY

Madrigalia: New & Selected Poems

Orexia

Satin Cash

Vanitas, Rough

Blue Venus

Glass Town

POETRY ANTHOLOGIES
(as editor)

*More Truly & More Strange:
100 Contemporary American Self-Portrait Poems*

Monticello in Mind: Fifty Contemporary Poems on Jefferson

All That Mighty Heart: London Poems

Acquainted with the Night: Insomnia Poems

LITERARY CRITICISM

The Hide-and-Seek Muse: Annotations of Contemporary Poetry

Paradise
Close

A NOVEL

Lisa Russ Spaar

A Karen & Michael Braziller Book
PERSEA BOOKS / NEW YORK

Copyright © 2022 by Lisa Russ Spaar
All rights reserved. No part of this may be reproduced or
transmitted in any form or by any means, electronic or mechanic,
including photocopy, recording, or any information storage and retrieval
system, without prior permission in writing from the publisher.
Request for permission to reprint or make copies, and for any
other information, should be addressed to the publisher:

Persea Books, Inc.
90 Broad Street
New York, NY 10004

Library of Congress Cataloging-in-Publication Data
Names: Spaar, Lisa Russ, author.
Title: Paradise close: a novel / Lisa Russ Spaar.
Description: First Edition. | New York: A Karen & Michael Braziller Book / Persea Books, [2022] | Summary: "In this novel, the seemingly unrelated tales of an anoretic 14 year old girl in 1971 and a reclusive, crestfallen man in 2016 entwine to show how the wages of the past are always with us, as are the dangerous and redemptive consequences of secrets confided and withheld"—Provided by publisher.
Identifiers: LCCN 2021048807 (print) | LCCN 2021048808 (ebook) |
ISBN 9780892555512 (hardcover) | ISBN 9780892556137 (paperback) |
ISBN 9780892555529 (ebook)
Classification: LCC PS3568.U7644 P37 2022 (print) |
LCC PS3568.U7644 (ebook) | DDC 813/.54—dc23
LC record available at https://lccn.loc.gov/2021048807
LC ebook record available at https://lccn.loc.gov/2021048808

This is a work of fiction. References to real people, events, or places
are used fictitiously. Other names, characters, places, and events
are products of the author's imagination, and any resemblance to
actual events, places, or persons, living or dead, is coincidental.

Designed by Rita Lascaro
Manufactured in the United States of America.
Printed on acid-free paper.

First paperback printing

for Sydney Hall Blair (1949–2016)

PARADISE CLOSE

PART ONE

The Close

The Close, February 1971

At about four o'clock in the afternoon, Marlise Schade, just shy of fifteen years old, stepped off a bus from Philadelphia, where she'd been living for the past six months on the adolescent wing of The Institute, a pricey psychiatric hospital that her guardian and her rapidly dwindling trust fund could no longer afford.

There had been only two other passengers on the bus with Marlise: a young woman in a drab winter coat and a boy about five years old. They sat near the front, but the boy, who held two pieces of Styrofoam that had been sloppily painted brown and red, presumably by the boy, maybe in a pre-school or at a kitchen table, kept wandering back to where Marlise sat by a window, her one bag wedged onto the seat beside her. The boy didn't speak. "You come back up here," said the woman from the front, without turning around.

"Hey, you," Marlise said to the boy. After a while, he backed away, keeping his big brown eyes fixed on Marlise, who crossed her bare legs and looked out the window. They were crossing the Ben Franklin Bridge, girders flipping past, the Delaware River slate and fathomless below.

The little boy stood now in the aisle beside the woman. "See," he said to her, leaning against her. "I have two doggies." He pressed the two pieces of Styrofoam together. "Kiss, kiss," he said. He threw his elbows into the woman's lap,

doggies in his fists, the Styrofoam squeaking, the boy making kissing sounds. The woman sighed. She adjusted the pocketbook in her lap, setting it upright, and stared out the window. Marlise convulsed with sadness. "I like your doggies," she whispered. Woman and child got off in Camden, and after that, except for the driver, Marlise had the bus to herself until she alighted at the Riverside depot.

Clutching her plaid coat about her, she shivered and sniffed: New Jersey. Engine exhaust. She studied the platform scum: bird lime, chewing gum, a condom flattened to the letter L. Snow blushed in patches around the station columns, and high over the Rancocas River, showing some skin through a slit of dark, opposite storefronts, the winter sky paled to emerald and glinted in the paisley swirls of parking lot potholes. Outside the Riverside bus station, with its vestigial, nineteenth-century scrollwork, she, Marlise Schade, stood alone, stamping her cowboy boots for warmth, waiting in the coach bay.

Her bare legs were cold, and she glanced down self-consciously at the filigree of black markings that trellised up her thin calves and thighs.

It had been Silas's idea, the evening before, her last night at the Institute, to have a makeshift farewell party for her, since the decision to move her had been so sudden. He'd somehow procured a black laundry marker and invited everyone who dropped by his room that evening to write a message or leave an autograph on Marlise's legs, arms, and hands. "I always thought I'd see you again," someone had written. That song. "Marlise leaves the Plaza!" someone else had scribbled on her right shin, with a pretty recognizable drawing of Marlise as Eloise, from the children's picture book, in short skirt and

suspenders, trailing a tiny turtle on a leash. The turtle looked like Silas.

Someone had managed to procure a tray of pot brownies that the party guests, coming and going from Silas's room (he had one of two single rooms on the ward), scooped out with their fingers in gooey wads—no sharps allowed inside, of course. And though Marlise herself didn't partake, she could still feel, stranded on the cold station platform, the chocolately lip-smear of Silas's kiss somewhere way up her inner thigh.

It had gotten late, and after a while, Seth, one of the shift orderlies, came and broke things up. He blew out and carted off the two guttering pillar candles that Silas had also managed to lift from the art room, the empty brownie pan, and told everyone to get to bed. Patients moved off down the dimmed ward hallway, in singles and in pairs. Marlise returned to her room where she threw a few things into a suitcase. When she'd first arrived, half a year ago, she'd been so unhappy that she'd refused to unpack anything she'd brought with her from boarding school. Now she was leaving almost everything behind.

Early the following morning, Phil, one of the nurses, escorted her down to the nursing station, where Marlise's godfather Maurice had already filled out the necessary paperwork for her discharge. Phil handed Marlise a one-way bus ticket. "You have just enough time to attend morning meeting," she said, stapling some papers together. "Then Seth is going to drive you to the station where you'll catch your bus. Bus will stop in Camden first to let people off. Just stay on it."

Where was Silas? Almost everyone else had been in the common room, updating the group on their progress in

therapy, sharing, or sitting, yawning, staring at the wall, the ceiling. Smell of oatmeal, toast, orange juice from the adjacent dining room. Surely Silas would come to see her off. He did not. Not even when Phil announced that Marlise was leaving that very morning, and everyone clapped. And now, standing in the February dusk, marked beneath her skirt by his smeary cannabis kiss, she felt his absence tear through her torso. She thought of the boy on the bus. Again, she clutched at her coat. She stamped her feet.

Before long, a pick-up rattled up beside the curb. A stout, stooped man in coveralls emerged. "Windy Bill," he said, by way of introduction, glancing down at Marlise's bare legs, and then "Seen you the day you was christened," hoisting her green valise into the truck bed and opening the passenger door so she could climb up.

Marlise had found it hard to form words the last few days. Drained and grateful for the silence, she leaned back into the scratchy seat of the overheated cab, its faint smell of cigarettes and fish.

Outside the truck, a blur: small bakery with a black and white-striped awning, a car lot roped off by tattered pennants. A stone pile of a bar called The Castle, its neon sign, a martini glass, already lit, scarlet pimento in a lone olive flickering on and off, on and off. Two more blocks of brick warehouses, one with blackened letters, THE WATCHCASE, and another, once a nylon stocking factory, now shuttered, mildew-tracked real estate signs in broken panes, cornices thick with pigeons.

Windy Bill steered the truck across a graffiti-scribbled drawbridge into the township of Delanco. The Rancocas threaded below. Though the river was brackish and tidal,

a tributary that emptied just a mile or so below Riverside into the Delaware, it was rimmed with a margin of ice. Old snow clung to the curbs of the town's main strip—gas stations and narrow, asbestos-shingled Victorians, many with glass-louvered front porches and cheap lawn chairs out front, Christmas lights still dangling from lean-to garages and eaves. The truck sputtered by the old Camp Meeting, now housing the post office and a 7-Eleven, finally turning right and up along the river road, where the houses and shops thinned out to whiskey grass and swaths of sumac.

After a few miles, where the largest sycamore Marlise had ever seen loomed like a giant piece of cutlery, they took another right, crunching their slow way down a long, crushed-shell drive to a three-story brick house, built in the late 1700s, rebuilt sometime in the 1860s after a fire, and situated on a small rise two-hundred yards from the water—her great-great grandparents' homestead, Paradise Close.

It was a place of former prosperity—corn fields, orchards, a vineyard—where Marlise had once been carried in arms by her mother, Beatrice Schade, the mythic Bea, with a family hybrid peach named for her, the Beatrice Cross, though Marlise could not remember her long-dead mother, except as she surfaced in the one photograph Marlise possessed of her, with its white border and date stamp, 1955, skeptical eyes flickering in a heart-shaped face, a parasol balanced over her shoulder as she squinted into sunlight.

Ida, an ageless woman wearing men's trousers and a hat with earflaps, was waiting for Marlise at the house. Ida was, she said, a distant cousin by marriage to Marlise's mother on the Eble side. Marlise frowned. Words, words, how to keep

any of it straight? And Ida was saying that she remembered when Marlise was just a mite. "You still a mite," she had added, an eyebrow raised.

A widow, Ida lived a short ways up the Rancocas. Ida called the river "the creek," or really, "the crick," but said she still kept the empty homestead going for the one remaining, far-flung Schade, Bea's brother Cole, Marlise's uncle, who now lived in Virginia but still showed up occasionally, though more and more rarely, for estate matters of one sort or another. Surely Marlise had met her Uncle Cole? Ida asked.

Marlise shook her head. At some point, maybe, long ago, she had encountered Uncle Cole, before her parents had died, though she was just a baby then, and perhaps even once or twice after that, too, but try as she might Marlise could not recall one single thing about him.

Ida showed Marlise up two flights of dark stairs. On the landing, she paused and pointed to a wall, out of which swelled what appeared to be one-half of a tree trunk coming right up through a semicircle cut into the floor boards and disappearing into a similar hole cut in the ceiling. The other half of the tree must have been hidden on the other side of the stairwell, wherever that was. The plastered walls of the landing were papered, a trellised willow pattern faded and coming unglued in resinous spots. No one had bothered to paint the tree trunk, and most of the bark was worn away, the exposed trunk black and smooth. "Yes indeed," Ida was saying, "it's just what it looks like. One of your people, long ago, built this house right up around the thing, couldn't bear to cut it down, I suppose. Pear tree, I think. Well over a hundred years old when the house was built, and survived a fire, too. Got to be long dead now."

The tree, Marlise wondered. Had it blossomed and borne fruit after the house went up around it? How long could it have lived without light, the roots drawing up what groundwater they could from the nearby river? Ida, meanwhile, was leading Marlise up another short stack of stairs into a warm, cramped space in the third story, chiseled with three deep dormers, a made-up twin bed, sheets, a blanket, two slip-covered pillows, and a washstand, topped with bowl and pitcher—a tidy, spare room just beneath the attic and overlooking the water, visible through the bare tops of plane trees still bristling with a few seed pods, silhouetted against the sun sinking now over the river. Maces, Marlise thought. The word for those little weapons.

Beside the bed stood a brass floor lamp, its silk shade shaped like a pumpkin, dangling with five gold tassels, each about eight inches long. "Looks like it don't, but it works," said Ida, reaching beneath the shade and clicking a switch. Saffron light suffused the dimming room. "Bathroom's down the hall," Ida went on, tapping a clanking radiator twice as though to make sure it was giving off heat. She would bring food at the start of each week, she had said, "and do walk over and see me at the marina if you need anything at all." She said it atall. Anything atall.

Marlise tried to concentrate. Who *was* Ida, exactly? And what marina? Food coming once a week. What day was it? Marlise was still picturing the blackened tree in-grown on the landing below, strange totem. Tomorrow she would slip back down the stairs and see if she could get her arms around the thing. What had those early builders done with all the branches? Did pear trees grow that tall? She pictured drupes of blasted fruits in rooms she couldn't see, ovaries wizened.

The bed of Odysseus and Penelope—was that right? Made out of a tree rooted in the earth? And it was their secret? And the answer to some sort of riddle? Or was she misremembering? Meantime, "Just got me a new owl," Ida was saying, putting a stack of folded bath towels on the cot and giving it a pat. "One wing nipped half off. Windy Bill spotted her in the Delta Grove one evening. Snatched her for me in a blanket. Bill knows, I'm partial to owls. I keep her in a wire cage now, back of my house."

From the upstairs window, Marlise watched Ida tramp off, sturdy in a barn coat, unfastened galoshes flopping at her ankles, trailing breath-scraps. The oyster-shell lane was pearly in the dusk, with a few ridges of rime as the path, and Ida with it, disappeared toward the packing sheds, orchards, old vineyard slope, the blackening suggestion of woods beyond.

Should she have asked Ida about a key, Marlise wondered. A key to the house? Houses had keys, right? Even houses with trees inside them. It had been so long since she'd been anywhere she hadn't been safely locked inside. Had Ida locked the door on her way out?

Marlise was too tired to make her way back down all those stairs to check. She leaned her forehead against the cold window glass, warmth from the gurgling radiator in the room at her back. Jet trails scored the sky overhead and, a far, far way off, way down the river, a sprinkle of headlights, cars passing over the water on the Route 130 bridge as night at last descended.

Marlise had just the one Samsonite suitcase, which she left unopened beside the bed. Not much in there. Her mother's copy of *Jane Eyre* with her autograph, *Beatrice Schade*, written inside the front cover in the deliberate, curlicue script of early

adolescence. Marlise's *Beggars Banquet* LP. Nothing to play that on now. In the hectic, hurried state in which she'd departed, she'd left most of her clothing behind. What would the orderlies do with it, she wondered. And who now slept in her bed there in room 7? From her orange leather shoulder bag she withdrew a joint and pack of matches printed with "Kelly's Seafood" on the cover, a parting gift from Silas. She smoked half of the joint, then lay down on the floor and slept.

The Institute, September 1970

The evening snack was over and some patients had already gone to bed. Others watched a small television set up in the common room. The music piping in was low-key and the lights had been dimmed, as they always were after ten, though it never got completely dark inside that place.

Then Silas Newman blew into the ward, a dervish of cannabis and autumn's shiver, an easel under one arm and a paint-spackled duffel bag stuffed with brushes, solvents, and tubes of oil colors in the other hand. Even the evening shift aides took notice, italicized by his energy, his classic features, long, lustrous hair, the braided silver toggles of his pea coat bristling with leaf-smoke and the sharp season. And now Silas was hugging everybody, greeting each stranger—patient or attendant—as his oldest, dearest friend. That enchanting voice, his full lips. Hair a smoky tousle, mouth dank and sweet. Lit.

Partially cracked doors began opening wider along the hallway, and two nurses stood watching, silhouetted at the threshold of their fluorescent station. Within moments he was surrounded. Eyes shone all around the dusky common room. *Wolves to a fire*, thought Marlise.

Younger than the rest of them, practically invisible most of the time, Marlise also watched Silas from a shadowy corner where she sat cross-legged on the floor with the ward copy of *The Complete Plays of William Shakespeare* opened in her lap. Nina the Nympho was sidling up the hallway toward the

As you like it, act II scene I

crowded room, Marlise noted. She turned her attention back to the page, where Duke Senior was talking with his men as they entered the forest of Arden.

> Now, my co-mates and brothers in exile,
> Hath not old custom made this life more sweet
> Than that of painted pomp? Are not these woods
> More free from peril than the envious court?

But Silas had spotted her after all, pile of twigs on the floor in the corner. She sensed this without looking up. If it had been possible to look down from the ceiling in that moment, at bird- or dream-flight height, she'd have seen the milling clutch of ragtag patients parting for him like the waters of the Red Sea in that Bible movie, as he approached in an aura of weed and linseed oil.

She stared down at the page. The muddy hems of his velveteen, flared pants and his heavy square-toed boots stopped in front of her. When he knelt down, she realized that he wasn't very tall. Rough outside air still hung about his coat. She inhaled. She wanted to swallow, but couldn't. He crouched, elbows on his knees, hands clasped between them, fingernails black.

He glanced at the book in her lap, then put his lips to her ear, wet and soft, though she felt his teeth. "Here," he said, without turning his face from her but sweeping one arm out behind him to acknowledge and encompass the room and all its galvanized denizens, "here, on the *inside,* we feel not the penalty of Adam."

"Nor," she said, without skipping a beat or casting her eyes at the page in her lap, but looking instead right up into his

startling face, finishing the lines for him, "the season's difference, as the icy fang, and churlish chiding of the winter's wind."

He paused. Had she surprised him? A suck of breath, then his face opening. An irresistible smile. "Dearest of all!" he whispered, before standing, turning, and the room reclaimed him.

Dearest of all. Of all what? She would turn the phrase over and over in her mind, later. How utterly pretentious, how presumptuous, she thought. Yet she could not stop herself from savoring its husky threat, the thrill of having been seen.

*

Dr. Lance, finger pads pressed each to each, eyes half-cast in his dimly lit office, had said to Marlise, "you are fourteen but you have the lusterless eyes and body of a crone." And other things like that, to shock. To get a rise. Was it that she didn't care? No. But her mind wasn't right, kept clouding up, her mouth dull, and the kinds of things she was invited to reveal had to do with a past with which she felt no connection, at least not one that she could put into words.

Once, when she'd walked over from the North Building for her daily appointment (what Silas, later, would call her "lance-ing") in the main Institute mansion, which looked a little like Tara from *Gone with the Wind*, and was waiting in the gloom of Dr. L's leather chairs and kelim pillows, his South American artifacts, she'd read a description of herself on a notepad on his desk, but obviously intentionally arranged so that she could see it from her seat—good grief, Marlise thought, it's all so transparent—an account in Lance-a-lot or some lackey therapist's briary scrawl of how at group therapy she, Marlise, would sit yoga-style, silently, and spit

her saliva into tissues, sometimes even slipping mouthfuls to the floor, not once appearing to swallow. All true, of course, but Marlise refused to react. Instead, she settled back into the large chair, yawned, and closed her eyes. By then she knew that two-way mirrors were everywhere.

The nurses and aides had loved her, though. Infantilized her. She let them. She was young and simply starving, far less trouble for them than the heroin addicts, the nymphomaniac, the boy who wouldn't wash, with matted hair and eyeglasses glazed with prune juice, or urine, someone said, and who knows what else, the suicide threats, the schizophrenics who came in manic, raving and riveting the ward like wind, or those on bad acid trips, one talking in rhyme, some of them balling one another in their rooms, the laundry, climbing the furniture and latticed sunroom partition, but who within a week, stunned on thorazine or stellazine, would hug the walls with shuffling feet. For them, the many locked doors, the barred windows, were redundancies.

Get it together, the staff would say. Get your head together now. Come down. At her last morning meeting, on the very February day she'd been driven to the bus terminal, Marco had shared with the group that he had remembered in therapy that his mother had tried to drown him. His doctor beamed. People applauded.

The Irish girl with the beaver coat was long gone by then. The girl—what was her name? Brianna? Bonnie?—had loaned Marlise the dank pelt, a junk store find or family relic, to wear on her daily walks that late fall, Marlise hymn-singing things she'd learned in chapel long ago, at school, circling the fenced-in grounds, the air burnt with institutional dinners and laundry from large smokestacks. *A thousand ages*

in thy sight are like an evening gone, and so forth. One stretch took her past row houses under the El, linden trees ringed with fences, children who sometimes stared back at her through the bars from gold leaf-piles, their jump ropes dangling, before running off. Marlise wondered what they saw. A Hallowe'en skeleton in a shaggy coat? A ghost. Barely there.

The Irish girl had been broad-faced, freckled and tall, Main Line, a rich hippy, with the belonging of the beautiful and bored, in residence for just a few weeks, who knows why, to get her out of someone's way, perhaps, but how Marlise had admired her wide vacant eyes, her thighs stolid in pale robins egg-blue jeans, her musk of sure flesh. The beaver coat, heavy and napped, engulfed Marlise, kept her from feeling she might be blown away by the wind as she stalked the yard in circles, until one morning the Irish girl was gone, evaporated, taking the heft of her coat and her enviable gravity with her.

*

Silas interviewed himself sometimes, especially when he was in the early stages of a new hospital stay or new medication, alone in his room or in the shower, the drugs beginning their slow erosion, he felt, of his very cell structure, sludging up then dampening the fire in his brain.

Q: Why do you persist in believing you were born into a controllable world?
A: Wind instruments, bells, swept floors. Birds. Cages. Headstones.

Q: Are you a person?
A: In this one instance . . .

Q: Only one?
A: It is called the body.

Q: Why do you care about her?
A: I care that you ask me about her.

Q: Why her?
A: Because she is wasting.

Q: Wasting what?
A: Life. Body. Youth. Beauty. No words for it.

Q: What are you wasting?
A: Your time.

Nina was not the subject of this self-conducted interview. It was the other one, the girl who was disappearing, always with a book in her lap, open like a shield. A pelvic shield, he thought. But here was Nina, again, in his doorway, already unbuttoning her shirt, eyes fixed on him, twisted smile, little baby teeth. While he still had it in him, and before anyone noticed, he drew her into his room, where they fucked, without taking off their clothes, quickly and without speaking against the wall.

*

Meanwhile, in the bright refectory, pills in paper cups at meals, cones of salmon croquets, rice Marlise spit into paper napkins and stuffed into her socks, flushed later. Vanilla supplement drinks, creamy scarves frothing the sink, the white badge of grass outside her window, which only opened so much. Surely they knew she tossed them.

Rumors that James Taylor was living on a floor above the adolescent wing. Always his voice piping into the public rooms, *something in the way she moves*, or Neil Young, the Stones. Janis. Jimi and Janis both dead that fall. One night, she'd been flooded along, AWOL, with others to a Sly and the Family Stone concert at the Spectrum. On regular nights she'd help Jo, the night aide, assemble the evening snack she wouldn't eat: vats of peanut butter, toast, the gleaming kitchen, smell of church suppers and bleach, that stainless steel vault a kind of chapel itself. Jo in her military hospital uniform, Jo with the sharp, weathered face of a man, who cut Marlise's hair, wisps like milkweed floss, in her room, methadone roommate passed out on the other bed, Jo brushing the snippets off of Marlise's shoulders, tenderly pausing over their knobs and keys. In Occupational Therapy, all those leather-fringed moccasins and belts, pre-cut from patterns. Pillar candles. Macramé plant holders. Where each afternoon until she was released, a girl, whose North Philly parents had her locked up for loving a black boy, would type "I want to live with a Cinnamon Girl" on the art room Underwood. "The rest of my life with a cinnamon girl."

*

"Dear Mother & Father, You should see the way flies swarm the bins behind the loading docks and laundry here at Ye Olde Institute. Heaps of sullied linens, discarded dinners. How do I see this, you may ask. Why? For one thing, people love *me* like that. They flock to me that way, like maggots. And I'm given free rein here, you must know that. Rein. Reign, haha! I hope this doesn't upset you. After all the times. After all. I go where I please. Does that alarm? Even as the year dies,

days shorten, and the country goes to mother fucking shit, they flock and feed. I'm needed here. By now <u>Lake Geneva</u> will be gelid where you are, & the Christmas fairs! & your galleries and rooms all alight, and Sister's pricey art shows, the spiced wine in copper vats & fresh horse dung in the streets!!! Well, I intend my own garden here. I tend. Yes, a garden. She is in need of me. Imagine. Me with a garden. Of course I speak in metaphor. I hope this does not seem to you <u>crazy</u> in any way. I have many plans. For my paintings. Which may seem useless to you. But what is 'useless'? Consider the lilies, &c. Does He not feed & clothe them as well as you & me, &c?!! Do not forget them, then, and this, sent with greetings, from the Inside, from your <u>Orphan,</u> your Lily Boy of the Field, Silas."

*

The nurses, smoking in the evenings in their crisp white caps and mini-skirts, their tall white boots, would stroke Marlise's hair, her bones. "Did you love your mother?" the multiple-choice psychological tests asked. Marlise puzzled over these paper questionnaire booklets in the day room, pencil in hand. I never knew my mother, how do I know if I love her. Or, I *love* her. If I say I "loved" her, does it mean I no longer do? The rigid tense infuriated Marlise. "Did you love your father?" Impossible to answer that one, her mother and her father having died together in a car wreck, a fairy story, when Marlise was just a baby. No questions on those tests about orphans, or about guardians and god-parents, but Marlise always thought of <u>Maurice</u>, who was both her guardian and her godfather, when she blacked-in any circle for "no."

In her first weeks at The Institute, Marlise spent her days moving, burning, burning, walking the paths that looped

around the locked courtyard. When she couldn't be outdoors, she jogged up and down the hallway. When her roommate was at therapy or out in the day room, she jumped on the bed like a child. Finally tired, she would sit, usually in some corner on the floor, orant, to read whatever she could find on the adolescent ward's one shelf of books—*Call of the Wild*, a Webster's dictionary, *Girl of the Limberlost*. *Valley of the Dolls*. *To Sir, With Love*. Two tattered editions of Shakespeare. What doctor's child's shelves had been raided for this motley library, she wondered. And at first there had been not only the many psychological tests and quizzes to puzzle over, but interviews with a series of nutritionists and student therapists. Marlise had shocked a psych resident when she said she pulled her own scant feces from her body with her finger. A ring of pimples around the white coat's quavering mouth murmuring "I see."

Then Silas had roared into her world. She unpacked her suitcase at last.

*

After that performance on his first night, when he'd whiplashed into the Adolescent Wing and shivered through the place, Silas seemed to have disappeared from the ward. Marlise was reluctant to admit that she was hoping to see him again. Where was he? She didn't even know his name and refused to ask anyone, lest she betray her interest. Had he disappeared, discharged as swiftly as he'd been admitted, like the girl with the beaver coat?

Marlise was beginning to realize that there was something that happened, especially to the manic ones. They came in on fire, leaping onto couches, spouting verse, ranting,

shedding clothes, but after about a week on horse tranquilizers, these same prophets became shades, shuffling, hugging the walls, monosyllabic, catatonic with runny noses in the morning meetings, hands hanging useless as the pendulums of broken clocks.

Silas had stirred her. And from her various hiding places—corners, the floor, the typewriter table in the OT room, or at the margins of the refectory where she picked at food, or in the outdoor courtyard with its fringe of fenced-in privet, yews, and hollies, its benches, walking, walking, sometimes jogging, often armed with one book or another—she'd kept an eye out for him.

*

It was Silas who found Marlise, sitting cross-legged on a chair in front of one of the art room typewriters, a blank sheet of paper rolled onto the platen, listening to the music piped in through ceiling speakers. Always, to Marlise, the lyrics seemed to be about food—black-eyed peas, peaches, fatback—could that be right?—when arms and a strong smell of sweat and stand oil wrapped around her from behind, smudged shapely fingers reaching to the keys to type out "Do you believe this LOAD OF SHIT place is really going to help you" on the blank sheet of paper emerging white and crisp as a surrender flag from the little machine.

Solvents, sweat, cannabis. Where did he manage to get it?

Without turning around, Marlise thought to type, "About time," but paused, then tapped instead, "TAKE ME TO YOUR LEADER, ALIEN VISITOR."

Then they'd typed their names onto the sheet of paper. She clacked out "Marlise Schade" and pushed the carriage return.

leaning in closer, arms still around her, tapped out, on a new line, right beneath her name, "Silas Newman." "Ah, little bird," he'd exclaimed "your first name holds mine!"

"Not quite," she typed.

A little later, after Silas had wandered back to his easel, Marlise tugged the piece of paper out of the machine, folded it into a small triangle, and tucked it into a front pocket of her carpenter's pants.

A few days passed, then, without a sign of Silas, during which time she felt unaccustomedly bereft.

One dawn she woke to find him sitting on the edge of her bed. Her roommate was still asleep on the matching twin across the room. Weak light striped the curtain of his hair as he bent toward her. "Come," he whispered, shoving aside the covers and helping her pull on and button up a pair of corduroy jeans. She had been too groggy to wonder at the ease and tenderness with which he did this, and only later thought too, with a flame of vanity and shame, what he'd thought of her thin bare legs, startled hip bones, concave belly, her negligible body.

They made their way down the quiet ward, his hand at her elbow. A few early risers, patients, orderlies passed them. A clanking of pots and pans came from the distant kitchen. Odor of bland oatmeal, powdered eggs, toast, cinnamon. Weak coffee. The nurse's neon station buzzed weakly at the far end of the hall. Opposite, down the dim corridor, was an open space, a sunroom, windows latticed with metal grids. "Come my lady," Silas said. "My hothouse flower. Survey your realm."

Shivering, faces pressed against the window panes, they'd peered out between the eyelet grill-work over the loading

docks below, the avenues of brownstones beyond the yard's metal fencing, amber haze of bolled trees, the streets adrift with red and yellow leaves. Sirens. Traffic. Rosy, lazy clouds. Two birds flitted past, lit by sun. The surf of the outside world. Seams of cold seeped through the grout. "Can you taste the seawater in your mouth?" he asked. She looked at him. "You are so beautiful," he said. She did not know what to say.

After that morning, Silas and Marlise had been more or less inseparable, finding each other in the mornings, and parting only when they had to or needed to—therapy sessions, sleep, her walks, reading, his time in the art room, painting. She thought he probably did things, sexual things, at least at first, with other patients. There was a constant circle of desperate eyes around him now that he had reappeared from his initial druggy, post-admitted stage. Nina, Marlise noted, was always hanging around his bedroom door, edgy, nervous, stepping in and out over the threshold. But eventually the ward settled down and stopped vying so hard for his attention, Nina appeared to take her affections elsewhere, and Marlise wondered that if by attaching himself as a kind of protector to her, the ward baby, seemingly fragile and lonely, he was shielding himself from his own ferocious magnetism, the almost out of control power he had over others and himself.

It was the most coherent thought she'd had in months.

The Close, February 1971

Marlise had loved her first weeks alone in the old family house. Most of the rooms were nearly empty; what little furniture was there was sheeted. She ran through the rooms, up and down the stairs, pausing briefly on the landing to stroke the dead, protruding pear tree. She avoided the cellar, where she imagined the ancient tree was rooted, and the attic, where surely its druidic top still branched skyward or had, ages ago, toppled into ruin. She pictured it, by turns, withered and diminished, with rotten fruit hung like bats, or still mysteriously fragrant, like the walking staff of Joseph of Arimathea that the nuns told her still bloomed where he stuck it into the pagan ground, somewhere in England.

She jogged in place. Did sit-ups. Jumping jacks. The old floors shook. She took long hot baths in a deep, claw-footed tub, the water rusty at first, then clear. The bathroom was almost as big as the bedroom. A bar of soap on the ledge was smooth and gray as stone. Sometimes she sat and pressed the ladder bones of her spine against the warm radiator, gazing across the room and out into the intricate tops of trees toward the river she knew was there, glinting, but could not see from the floor. When she thought at all, it was about what these rooms had been like before she had come to them, so long abandoned and unpeopled, crossed by draperies of light and shadow, tree branch, startle-scissor of birds, the mystical speech of geese.

In the kitchen, she nibbled from waxed paper sleeves the Saltine crackers which Ida brought. Marlise keyed open tins of sardines, sucking the oil from her fingers. The little silver fish and bones, the cans of tuna, she fed to the barn cats that haunted the side porch, which was as far as she ventured outside before backing into the kitchen and turning the deadbolt. She poured the cats milk, too, in teacups. Fed them the potatoes and noodles from the soups Ida bought or made, saving for herself the translucent slivers of broth-suffused celery, onion, tomato. She'd carry the box of cereal upstairs, tonguing a few flakes, setting the rest out an opened window onto a wide sill until the birds came regularly, sometimes tapping the glass with china beaks—chickadees, nuthatches, titmice, once a grosbeak she had to identify with a book of Northeastern Songbirds she'd found in a glassed-in bookcase downstairs.

She'd also discovered two children's books, perhaps once belonging to her mother and uncle, one about a boy combing the shore for seashells, with illustrations—scallop, cat's cradle, mussel, conch—who comes upon a beached whale, and the other about Children of Foreign Lands. Boys and girls in kimonos. Wooden clogs. Feather head-dresses. Saris. Serapes. These she took upstairs to her room. The marvelous papery lampshade gave off a burning smell, so she removed it, setting it in a dormer sill, and read by a bare bulb. Sometimes in the dark, in bed, inside one of the nightgowns that was in the box of clothes that had come from Maurice soon after she'd arrived, cast-offs, she guessed, from some step-daughter or another, she'd hear geese lowering over the rooftop toward the river, their migratory thonking coming from right up inside her own frail vest of bone.

The Institute, November 1970

"What do you remember about your childhood," Dr. Lance asked Marlise. "Anything. The smallest detail." Her mind towered, blank as cloud. Her first school, benign enough, hallways, beds in a row for the girls like her, who boarded during the weekdays. Daytime naps on floor mats. Sour milk. Small animals treading air in wire wheels above cedar chips in little cages. Cards above the blackboard showing how to make the letters she practiced drawing over and over on ruled paper. Chapel on Thursdays. Talk of God the Father, an abstraction as remote and unlikely to Marlise as parents, though she bowed her head and prayed.

Maurice, mildly affable, dutiful, distant godfather, still lived in Haddonfield then, and she spent weekends and vacations with him and his family, but a few years ago he'd moved to a stone farmhouse in Bucks County. He'd had a series of pretty wives, a host of wary step-children, one of whom, a girl about her own age, had fingered her when they shared a bunk bed on a family stay at the shore. Was she supposed to feel something as the older girl pushed two fingers up inside her? "Don't you want to?" the girl had asked. "Look, I'll show you how, silly," taking Marlise's hand and slipping it under the elastic waistband of the older girl's pajama bottoms. Hair there where Marlise had none yet. Grains of sand in the sheets, the girl's larger hand on top of Marlise's, pushing her fingers down on top of the digits like piano keys, the older

girl hot inside, wet, as she writhed and made small grunts, squeezing Marlise's fingers with her body. Then she pulled Marlise's hand away, rolled on her side, back to Marlise, and almost immediately began to snore. Fingers sticky, Marlise wiped them on the bedsheets. Later, she climbed out of the bed and made a pallet on the floor. Staring at the ceiling, she tried again, on herself, using the other hand. Nothing. She wanted to cry. When she woke up, it was morning. The other girl stood over her in a swim suit, then spun around and laughed on her way out the bedroom door. "You'll be okay, Marly Baby," she'd said. Marlise lay still on the floor, the rental house around her already smelling of the new day's bacon, maple syrup, and suntan oil.

Marlise told none of this to Dr. Lance. "I remember Miss Olensky," she said. The school librarian, who had shown her the Little House books, the "signature" biographies of the queens, the war nurses, the authors. Then later, real teachers showed her the writers who became her other teachers, opened worlds where orphans triumphed, *Reader, I married him*, but where, too, you could be shut up, fatally, in Prose. *It would have starved a gnat to live as small as I.* Or a posse of other lost children could crush your eyeglasses and kill you.

"Do you remember your mother and father?" Dr. Lance had asked.

Her father, not at all. He was a figment she'd mapped onto Maurice and her Uncle Cole, whom she could not recall ever meeting, though surely she had met him, her dead mother's brother, the heir of Paradise Close, everyone else in the immediate family dead now, an oddball, who owned lots of properties he refused to repair or abandon completely. When Silas had suggested to her that Maurice might actually be her

real father, Marlise had struck him on the mouth. Which had surprised them both, split his lip, and made him bleed. They both had laughed, dabbing at the scarlet blood with tissues. But this possibility was something that had also crossed her mind, and more than once. Why else would Maurice have been so doggedly devoted to her, in his remote and bumbling way, despite all of his own draining domestic and financial entanglements?

Once she'd dreamt that Dr. Lance was her father, helping her learn to tie her shoes, bent at her feet. "I remember my mother with an umbrella," she offered. "What color was it?" Dr. Lance had asked. "Cochineal," she lied, savoring the word. The photograph she possessed was black and white. And after all, Marlise was barely three when the car her father was driving slid on a sheet of black ice into the sludgy deeps of the Raritan Canal and drowned both parents. She recalled nothing about the funeral, and not much after that, either.

"Who are you, then," Silas had asked at one point, his arm draped around her shoulder. They were on a sofa in the common room, where one of the nurses was wrapping a string of colored lights around an artificial Christmas tree though Thanksgiving was still a week away. Marlise felt the world sliding inexorably from equinox to the extremes of solstice.

"I'm Ignorance," she'd said, "and Want."

"That's Dickens," he said. "Not you."

They sat for a while in silence, Silas stroking her arms, nuzzling her ears, nibbling her neck. "Schade. Marlise Schade," he said. "You know, in German, *schade* means 'bad.'"

"Too bad," she'd said.

Bucks County, Thanksgiving 1970

Marlise still hid and threw away food, but she seemed well enough to Dr. Lance by Thanksgiving—up to nearly 90 pounds—to make the trip to Bucks County for the long holiday weekend. Since Silas had no place to go (his parents were living abroad somewhere, Montreaux, he thought, or perhaps visiting his sister the gallery manager in Paris), Marlise had convinced Maurice to consent to Silas's coming along for the holiday. What's one more? Maurice had said, but Marlise heard the fatigue and smoke in his voice as it crackled through the receiver of the ward's hallway payphone.

It had been a bad idea. By Friday evening, Silas had discovered and smoked an entire dime bag belonging to the son of Maurice's current wife, Sylvie, and was later caught with his hand up the shirt of one of her daughters in the master bedroom linen closet. Hearing about this pained Marlise. What was Silas to her? Brother? Caretaker? Antic force? Who or what was she to him?

But before that, before Maurice had driven them both back to The Institute on Saturday, earlier than planned, there had been that bitingly cold Thanksgiving Day afternoon when Sylvie, on her last legs with Maurice, and who apparently had some kind of guru back in London, had gone up to a rocky field behind the house to spray-paint a labyrinth onto the dun grasses. First she had tied red ribbons in various trees and shrubs to symbolize her unmet spiritual wishes and

future desires, but while she was mapping out her labyrinth, following directions from a sheet of paper and pointing a can of rust-red spray paint at the ground, pacing out her steps, a herd of cows that had busted loose from a neighboring farm had circled her. Their breath chuffed the air, their scrutiny sullen. Terrified, she began to call for help.

By the time Maurice, Silas, Marlise, and some stepchildren and neighbors had gathered at the hilltop, Sylvie was in a heap, sobbing on the ground. A few yards off, a calf chewed placidly on one of the red ribbons as the rest of the herd mulled about in steam, mud, and piss. "Look, Maurice," Sylvie spat out, syllable by syllable, her fit of weeping arrested by the embarrassed stares of the onlookers. "At least the fucking labyrinth is completely clear. At least the bitches didn't shit in the labyrinth."

"Shit in the labyrinth" became Marlise and Silas's code phrase after that. Most of the formulations were his idea. Formation of the United States Environmental Protection Agency as Oyster Creek Nuclear Facility opened 40 miles from Philadelphia? Shit in the Labyrinth. Someone taping "out of order" signs on all the payphones during the Institute Christmas party (Silas pretended to make several loud and querulous overseas calls to his parents, just to show he wasn't fooled)? Shit. Philly Police Commissioner Rizzo raids the Black Panther Offices and strips their "black asses" in the street? Shit in the Labyrinth. Silas, beautiful Silas, small and compact but full of lips with long, lustrous hair, Silas of the breath-taking, hairless chest, Silas of the racing mind, heading for the basement shock rooms? Shit. Marlise, unformed, sprung into a parentless, impoverished, unsupervised limbo while still in the helpless throes of self-starvation? Shit. Shit in the effing labyrinth.

Philadelphia, February 1971

Maurice, her godfather, had driven down from Bucks County and taken her to La Terrasse for lunch, as he always did, dutiful, good—or, well, *okay*, godfather-guardian—that he was, on his monthly visits during her past half year in The Institute.

She had to admit that he had been good about arranging for that, getting her out of boarding school at Barton and onto The Institute's Adolescent Psych Ward. Saving her life, as they say. No privacy, of course, and people—nutritionists, aides, shrinks—trying to get her to eat, to talk, to remember things. Group therapy. Psychodrama in the evenings, meetings she often skipped, all that hysterical role-playing—"James," the therapist would say, "you be Esther's mother. Now scream at her! Really scream. Yes, that's it, scream at her like it like you mean it. Now, Esther, how does it make you feel when James says she never wanted you to be born?" But Marlise found it much like school, a low level of protection, intrusion, and neglect, occasional cruelty, her own body in revolt.

Marlise had not been ready for Barton when, at the end of seventh grade, the time had come for her to switch schools. It was Sylvie who chose the place—recently co-ed, a tier below Choate and Phillips Exeter and those places, but respectable enough. And far enough away from Bucks County to make it appealing to a woman who didn't particularly want to share

any more of her already vexed domestic sphere with the bookish, spectral daughter of her husband's long-dead friend Beatrice Schade. His former lover, probably. Surely that was clear to everyone, though no one spoke of it?

Thinking back on the year she spent at Barton, Marlise realized that probably nothing especially unusual or even wrong had happened to her there amongst the other precocious, privileged, confused young people left largely to their own devices—some dope smoking, brief experimental sexual encounters, secret trips into the city and back before dawn and the start of field hockey practice or chapel or classes. Except for some pot-smoking, Marlise didn't participate. She watched and hid and listened. The problem was her body. The palms of her hands, her shins, hurting at night, breasts like welts, the blood that started, a private surprise of thrill and confusion, in the school's basement art room, her period coming on later for her than for other girls she knew—that was the difficulty, all of this helpless *change*, and all that it seemed to invite. In others, not herself. Her mother, beautiful Beatrice, squinting into the sun. Here is my body, gazing at yours. Feast.

Marlise, studious, quiet, still a girl in many ways, wanted to shut it all down but didn't know how—how to say no, how to balance the pull into smoky rooms smelling of jam and bong water with the lure of her school books and the art room with its drawing paper, calligraphy inks, dark-room privacy. And perhaps most of all, what to do about her erupting body and her own loneliness begging for attention?

Was it an accident, then, the fall she took, high one early summer night, under a crush of stars and someone's stereo playing, tumbling like an abject angel out a lower

story window into a hedge, concussing, breaking an ankle? On crutches for the better part of the next two months, hobbling in the heat of the mostly empty Barton campus, Marlise, already thin, had, from the exertion, dropped ten, then twenty pounds. At first she didn't notice, but in time she came to love the secret of it, the control, for once, that she could exert by skipping meals, watching as her knee and pelvic bones sharpened into view. Most of the other students were on family vacations; the staff was adjunct and reduced. Nobody paid much attention to her. It gave her a private high to be so light, so unburdened. Her breasts stopped burning. The monthly bleeding stopped.

By the time school was about to start up again in late August, and the headmaster phoned Maurice, Marlise—billeted in the school infirmary—was under 70 pounds, so lethargic she had to be transported to Philadelphia prone in the backseat of Maurice's Volvo station wagon. What had begun within her control had veered. She was burning off her body's protein. Her kidneys were about to fail.

So, yes, godfather Maurice had, in many ways, saved her. For two weeks at the end of August 1970, Marlise, whisked away from Barton at death's door, was in the regular hospital in Center City, on an IV, getting "recalibrated," as Maurice put it. Once she was stabilized they moved her over to the adolescent wing of The Institute, a modern tall-rise adjacent to the much older, original Hospital for the Insane in another part of Philadelphia, a residential hospital, one of the best adolescent facilities anywhere, Maurice had said. "I hear they play a lot of volleyball over there," one of the Center City hospital nurses had said, trying to prepare her for the transition.

It was true. Lots of volleyball. Lots of OT. Lots of walking. Talking. Daily therapy. Locks to anything outside. No completely closed rooms. No sharps.

But the money was running, *had* run out, Maurice was explaining, settling into his chair and ordering them both omelets and himself a bottle of 1960 Père Anselme Châteauneuf-du-Pape. *What* money, *whose*, Marlise had wondered as he continued, saying he was on his way that very evening to Las Vegas via Atlantic City. Maurice rubbed his eyes. Then on to San Francisco.

He smiled sadly at their waitress, dark nipples, braless beneath a gauzy white shirt. Black skirt. Marlise also studied her, a University of Pennsylvania student maybe, then scanned the brick floor. Winter sunlight touched everything, the white plates, silver forks. She liked this part, the feeling on the glassed-in patio of belonging neither to room nor to world entirely. Sometimes she wished she were a bird. But not so she could fly away.

Maurice was probably only 40-something, maybe closer to 50, and he was, or had been, a handsome man in a blue-blood way, but that afternoon his eyes were puffy, and he coughed as he chain-smoked. His nose and cheeks were blotchy. Marlise let him talk, his voice fading in and out of her attention, which was how things had been for her lately. Sylvie, the third wife, had finally moved back to London, and well, good riddance, he said. She'd milked him. He twisted a substantial gold pinky ring. He was flat out broke. Well, not flat out, but almost. "All relevant," he said. "I mean all relative. Relative. And fixable, sure." His grown sons by his first wife were still both gallivanting up and down the West Coast, one in a commune of some sort, wearing

bells, passing out leaflets in parking lots, squandering his Princeton education ommming at airports in saffron robes; they rarely called except for money. "So you see, honey, I'm sorry, I'm going to have to be away for a while, and for now it appears," he said, suppressing a cough, "that there's not enough left for school either. At least not for the tuition at Barton."

Maurice reached across the white tablecloth, its hamlet of glassware, to touch her plate, folded slab of omelet, fretted brown with bits of garlic, thyme, three spears of asparagus on the side. Cigarette between his fingers, he pushed the plate toward her a little. "Doctors say you're not quite ready to go back, anyway." Marlise held her napkin to her mouth. Into it she slipped an unswallowed bite of egg. Rush of chemicals in her brain, the suggestion of butter, fat. A contact high. Her pelvis clenched.

"I wrote your Uncle Cole, you know, he's off somewhere down south now, a hermit, lives in an abandoned restaurant or something, up along the Blue Ridge. And his secretary, Hilde it was for a long time, or someone else, maybe it was just him pretending to have a secretary, or it could have been one of his, ah, associates, anyway somebody wrote to say that you could, you know, stay on your mother's, his, the old farm over in Jersey, just until things get straightened out." Then, "It shouldn't be for too long." After a pause, "I'd heard he was going to sell the Close. Nobody left there, and he must need the money. But Cole just can't let go of—well, he's always been strange. Strange that way."

More silence, during which Marlise wondered if by "money" Maurice meant her alleged trust fund, set up by whom? Her Uncle Cole, she supposed, after her parents died,

to be used for her care and education until she became "of age." And whether that money was now all gone.

Marlise found it hard to form thoughts lately, to glean meaning, especially regarding matters pertaining to her family, herself, any kind of future, things they were always asking her to think about, back at The Institute. Sitting beside Silas sometimes, on the floor of the OT room, she'd marveled as he spun out to her exuberant concepts he had on his mind—"What does 'now' mean in a different place from here?" and "Do you think Time is something we live inside, or is it trapped inside us?" or "How is it that we only know the past but not the future?"—and she could feel his mind actually working, shaping these questions, whereas most of the time she felt that she could only react to things. If that. Had this always been true? How could she know, if she could not remember?

Maurice was still talking, low, apologetic. Usually he didn't talk this much. Marlise lifted her eyes from her plate. "Okay, look," he said. "I am sorry. Very, very sorry. Very. But you won't be on your own exactly. There are some people around there still, not him, don't worry, I might be worried if it were Cole, just because he's such a, a weirdo, but there are other people, old people, looking after, living on the place. They know you're coming. You'll be okay for a while, until I get back." More coughing. "Then we'll get you some therapy and into a public school, back at the books, eh, Brontë? Once you're better?"

Maurice sometimes called her Brontë because since girlhood she'd always had "her nose in a book," an interest that seemed both to puzzle and impress him. Finally, "Your mother, God, you have to know *I* loved her. We all did. She

was terrible, I mean *it* was terrible. What happened. Of course she was terribly beautiful. Tragic, what happened. And I do think, uh, I do think *she* would want you to know, she would want *me* to tell *you*, that women—girls, I mean—can stop um, *menstruating*"—at this word, he stumbled, and Marlise looked down at the table again, "they stop, they stop doing it *forever*. If they don't, well, you know, eat?"

The Institute, December 1970

Silas and Marlise were sitting side by side against a tiled wall of the OT room. Other patients and therapists milled about or sat motionless at craft tables under the fluorescent lights. This was the late afternoon hour for Occupational Therapy, before dinner, when people from all the wards gathered, not just the adolescents, and there were bent white heads among the darker ponytails, braids, and beards. Outside the trees were turning gold, orange, crimson.

Silas was small for a 20-year-old, about Marlise's height, with thick dark hair that hung about his extraordinary, feminine face, but seated he was taller than she was, and his shoulders were broad, his arms tendoned and strong. He was as old as he could be and still be kept on an adolescent ward, and he had been here before, when he was younger. He'd been hospitalized in some other places, too, before that. In and out, he said, since thirteen.

Marlise felt safe inside the thick cabled sweater he'd given her, saturated with the smell of him, like the wet wool of a sheep-studded vista in a castle tale on the morning after a great and cataclysmic event...

She was drifting again, "lucid dreaming," Silas called it, and shivered awake. Silas's lips were wet and pink, they always were, as though he smeared them with Vaseline, maybe he did, above them the slight brown down of a mustache.

Marlise stared as he spoke, holding up to the light a slide from a box in his lap.

"What about this one?" he asked excitedly. "Guess."

Marlise shook herself and peered into the little cellophane square with its cardboard frame. His hand had a slight tremor. The medication.

"I don't know," she said. What was she looking at? Something like a bloated, inverted gold heart taking up most of the slide, which depicted a canvas on a slivered background of black and deep green. The heart-shape was yellow, hazy, tropical, flecked with something, dragonflies, maybe? Dragons?

"Tolkien?" she said.

"No, no," he said. "It's John Mitchell. The bastard. Don't you see the copters? They're dropping over America! Ha, ha, but Tolkien, that's a good idea."

Marlise touched Silas's arm. She'd disappointed him, could feel his frustration with her. She knew little to nothing about the political issues and people that obsessed him. He was showing her slides, photos taken of a series of paintings he had done during the past two years, before he'd been readmitted. He called them the "Meat-Locker Torsos." Each canvas, he said, was about the size of the average adult human torso, and showed an open chest cavity, shoulders to waist. The idea was to suggest the identity of these headless and legless figures by depicting what made them tick. "Visible manifestations of soul. If these people have one, or what stands in for one," he said.

She'd guessed "your mother?" for "James Lovell," mistaking the astronaut's ropy cord floating across a fathomless field of deep indigo for an umbilicus.

They were marvelous, the canvases, as he held them up in miniature, celluloid copies, though she couldn't once surmise the identities correctly. The shadowy corridors of a ruined roman bath in cross-section—stairs, alcoves, hallways, lurking male figures clad in crimson—was the Pope. The gears and cogs of an autopsied long clock was St. Augustine ("I know what time is until someone asks me," Silas always liked to say). Two dove-gray lungs pelted with rain were meant to evoke the soggy insides of Silas's grandfather, who had drowned himself in the Danube, or so he'd been told. Eyeballs floating in a gray soupy sea were for Ivan Denisovich ("You know," said Silas, "from the Solzhenitsyn novel?"). One canvas showed two black, skeletal arms, elbow to fist, one emerging from each side of a scarlet canvas, the hands clutching one another in the middle, creating a double fist where the navel would have been on a real torso.

"Something about the Black Panthers?" Marlise had said.

"No, no, no. It's Emily Brontë!" he'd said, shoving the slide back into the box and jamming the lid back on top. "That's Heathcliff and Cathy, busted through their coffins, holding hands from beyond their graves."

Silas had shoved off after that, and she didn't see him for two days. Was it instinct, the pain she felt in disappointing him, that led her, at dawn a few days later, to the open door of the ward laundry room, gray and shadowy, where she'd found Silas slumped against the large industrial sink, arms up to the shoulders sunk under water? How had he gotten into that locked place? Why had she?—his clothes on the floor, a bloody dinner fork, thin ribbons of blood, red thread seeping from the small nicks in his wrists helixing up through the water, and she'd pulled him up into air by the armpits in her

own skeletal arms, screaming, screaming. After that, she had felt for nearly a week something push against her from the inside, like the soul they say enters us when we're born and lives within our bodies until we die.

*

While Silas was away getting stitched up and re-medicated at the main hospital, Margeaux, one of the occupational therapists, had confided in Marlise that Silas, now surely destined for shock therapy, already had something of a reputation as a painter. A prodigy. A painter's painter, she'd said. Marlise didn't know what that meant. He'd skipped high school, or gotten it all done quickly in a series of teaching hospitals and also, Margeaux thought, a special program for the arts in New York. He had even gone right into a famous art school in Rhode Island for a bit when he wasn't in hospitals.

Rummaging in a cupboard, Margeaux extracted a postcard. On one side, in tile format, were six images, each showing a woman's long neck wrapped with something different: a child's two fat, bluish arms; an oversized pocket watch with needle-like arrow hands stuck at midnight (or noon); a gilt-edged mirror capturing a lone wisp of cloud. One neck was itself a bottle of something cedar-tinged, like tea or scotch, with little sperm-like bodies floating in it. A large red beak. A breast, the nipple bleeding. On the other side, Marlise read "Choke-Her: Mother Paintings" and the name of a Philadelphia gallery, with an address and some dates.

Margeaux's boyfriend had been co-owner of a small gallery space, and they'd hosted a show for Silas when he was just sixteen. That was during his first hospitalization at The Institute. Back then, she said, the doctors had been much

more permissive with him, the wunderkind, allowing his parents to send him shipments of the German and Italian oil paints and solvents he liked to use, letting him stretch his own canvases, and giving him his own space and extended time to work in the OT art room. The show had gone well, drawn a decent crowd, and received a nice write-up about "the boy genius working with Rilkean 'thing-ness' in a faux naïf style," but none of the paintings had sold. And there had been a negative notice, too, along the lines of "immature, self-involved navel gazing, no better than the apprentice work of a beginning art student. Calling Dr. Freud!" This clipping, sheathed in a plastic folder, Margeaux had shown Marlise, as well.

Silas had been allowed to go to the opening, under Margeaux's supervision, and was exhilarated all evening, she said, sipping champagne and chatting up the crowd despite the fact that no one from his family had made an effort to be there. But a few days afterwards, Silas consumed some turpentine and was found unconscious in the ward shower. His father had flown in then from Europe to retrieve him from the main hospital where he'd been rushed to have his stomach pumped, and Margeaux had lost touch with Silas after that for a year or so, though her boyfriend, now her husband, had since sold some of the mother paintings, and was very interested in the torsos, which he'd seen only on the slides. But Silas was not interested in letting them go. "Silas has a mean streak, you know," Margeaux said. "Delusions of grandeur. Vindictive. He blames us for that bad review, can you believe that?"

Where were they at the moment, Marlise wondered, the actual canvases? All those paintings?

Silas, when he returned after his suicide attempt in the ward laundry, was heavily medicated, subdued at first. But he found Marlise and rebounded, and soon they were again inseparable, though never entirely alone, because of course Silas was now known by everyone to be not just charismatic, manic, and highly-strung, but a danger to himself. He was under much closer watch.

Virginia, March 1971

Cole Schade prided himself on his lingual skills, but try as he might, he could not make this young lady come. Climax. Achieve an orgasm. Whatever the youth were calling it these days. A German friend once called it "höchstewallung." Highest boiling. Over the mattress of his king-sized waterbed, a window mottled with dawn.

You lie there, then, and think of England, he thought. Or Nixon. Shrugging a little unsteadily up off the undulating bed, he reached for his khakis. Thank God he was much too old to be drafted. Unsuitable anyway, at any age. For anything. Lighting a Camel, he realized that Sally, or Sadie, yes, it was Sadie, waitress he'd met in town the night before, a student place where they served bad draft beer in mason jars. Sadie was passed out.

This saddened Cole. Though single all of his life, he loved women, their bodies, their power over him, and he especially enjoyed giving them pleasure orally, something he found that he couldn't ever talk about with the young men he knew in college and later in law school. The lovers he'd had over the years, while sometimes surprised, at first, by his insistence on making it the main part of every encounter, quickly accepted and then seemed to enjoy his obvious delight in their pleasure. He hoped they weren't faking it. Surely this was why Hilde had stayed with him for so long? He and she were both middle-aged, and their affair had gone on for over a decade.

Hilde had pointed out to Cole that while he spent a lot of attention on her, he was uncomfortable if she tried to reciprocate in a similar way. It's your hoarding thing, she'd said, with characteristic forthrightness. You don't want to give anything away. Even your jizz. She'd been right, of course. Cole missed her.

He glanced around the room, which had once been the main dining area in the former restaurant where he now lived. He looked up at a print framed behind water-spotted glass and hung crookedly over his chest of drawers. It was a copy of a drawing, maybe Picasso, done in pink and rose hues, a woman supine, eyes closed, one hand clutching the bedclothes, the dark head of a naked man or perhaps a woman between her parted legs. A cat looking on. Cole sighed. The painting had given him so much joy over the years. But there was something about these younger women he took up with—an indifference to sex, or at least to receiving pleasure? Was it concern elsewhere? Reduced attention span? Revulsion? He wasn't getting any younger, he knew that. He felt an urge sometimes to explain to them that there was nothing at all perfunctory or manipulative about this obsession of his. He pined to express it. Across the room, Sadie turned over in her sleep. The walls shimmered with light coming off the water bed.

Sadie must have slipped away, back to town, later that morning in the Datsun in which she'd trailed his old Jaguar the night before, relieved, no doubt, to find the old man gone when she'd surfaced on the ridiculous, floaty mattress. While she slept, he'd been out checking on the marble house, up the parkway, which he did every day, rain or shine, at exactly 10 AM. It was another property he had collected

over the years and then given back to the mountain rains and kudzu. For a while, before he purchased it, it had been a roadside attraction, stuccoed with thousands of marbles, the old-fashioned kind, aggies, bumblebees, jaspers. The whole place was filmed with grime now, mold and moss, birds and raccoons nesting in it, a warren of pests in there, no doubt, but in its prime the exterior could blind a person on a sunny day. Later it was turned into a "haunted house," created by the married pair who owned the place, with drivers touring the parkway stopping in to be terrified by the faux paper maché and chicken-wire ghosts of an old plantation owner and his enslaved mistress. Fake blood. Soundtrack of moans and cracking whips. Inappropriate, bizarre people.

But Cole got the whole thing, house and land, for almost nothing when the husband died and the wife was carted off somewhere by a relative. Before the end, though, the couple, in a fit of entrepreneurial ambition, had designed and erected a few large Styrofoam dinosaurs and positioned them in the bamboo canes that thronged the edges of the lawn and parking lot. There was, for a time, also a painted reproduction, Foam Henge, that stood about the height of a dray horse next to the small gravel parking lot. Cole occasionally came upon garishly painted chunks of it, stuck through with metal rods, rearing up underfoot when he was kicking around the grounds.

Now Cole, back at the restaurant, stood watching the long drive that snaked down to the parkway and interstate winking with cars and freight trucks in the overcast valley spread below. The sky was definitely darkening. Snow was on its rapid way from further south, despite its being early March. He was in the glass vestibule, a lobby off the now rutted and

weed-sprung parking lot, where there still hunched an old cigarette machine and where there had probably once been a rack for patrons' umbrellas, coats, and hats. Back in the day when people wore real hats and took them off when they came inside a restaurant. Now the entryway was stacked with brown paper grocery sacks crammed with things Cole hadn't yet figured out how to discard, newspapers, coupons he'd clipped for grocery stores in town, some of them over ten years old, rubber bands, aluminum foil balls, tuna fish cans he sometimes used for ash trays, but also in there somewhere the Daughters of the American Revolution papers his mother had once entrusted to him. Family photographs. Bonds, deeds of sale, title work, wills, other documents he really needed to sort through one of these days. Or so said Hilde, back when she still worked for him.

"You know," Hilde had said to him, the last time she had left him for the last time, "you're going to die under all of this stuff." She'd been inside, but was on her way out of the old dining area, cracked turquoise vinyl booths piled similarly with bulging paper bags, stacks of magazines, a welter of clocks, suitcases, cardboard boxes. His waterbed in a corner, shoved beneath a window where the waitress station had been. She'd collected up all her clothes and other woman things. Tubes, lipstick, shampoo, a hairbrush from the counter in the old restaurant Ladies Room, its stalls now door-less. Nylon stockings yanked from a towel rack. A box of Tampax. "You are going to be found someday when this crap falls over on you and crushes you to death," she said, her purse clicking shut. "And you'd better get rid of the cats. Cats whose owners die and can't feed them anymore? They eat their owners. A dog would sooner starve. Get a dog."

"Oh," she said, arms full and using a shoulder to push open the restaurant door on her way out, "please, please see a doctor."

That had been about a month ago. Cole felt that he was starting to lose track of time, and he didn't like it. At just that moment, his many clocks, long clocks, mantle clocks, cuckoo, grandfather, the ones that still worked anyway, whirred and clicked into gear, and began to chime the noon hour in the dining room behind him. Cole pulled up a shirtsleeve to reveal the large, raggedy blue-black mole growing on his right arm. He thought it looked more and more like the state of New Jersey. That was a sign of something. A hair sprouted from it, silver as what hair he had left, which he wore in a thin ponytail. He touched the mole to his lips twelve times. Then he touched each one of the lumps that had been swelling on his chest over the past year. Tumors, one doctor had said. Matter of time. Seven of them. He briefly pushed his fingers into each one.

Noon at last. Time for the day's first beer. And two hard-cooked eggs, which he boiled over a massive, grimy stove in an unwashed pot in the old restaurant kitchen for precisely ten minutes, and then cracked and ate, standing outside among the ten or so cats beside the grease pit out back, in all weather, despite rain or shine or, as was the case today, an oncoming blizzard apparently barreling up from the south. Despite the road trip north he'd been planning, for some time, to make that very afternoon.

The Close, March 1971

Marlise had another fat letter from Silas. That made seven in the nearly three weeks since she'd left the Institute and had been living alone in the house on the river. How did these envelopes find her, she wondered, scrawled simply with "Marlise Schade, Paradise Close, New Jersey."

She left this last one unopened on the top of the food box Ida had dropped off that morning, bearing the news that a March snowstorm, a blizzard maybe, brewing off the Carolinas, was heading rapidly north and inland. Windy Bill might not be able to get out to the store or post office for a bit, she said, if they got what they said was coming, his house on stilts out along the crick. Also, any proper plowing of the lane from the house out to the main road had been irregular since the man who rented the front fields to keep the property in Land Use only grew soybeans in the spring and summer, and drove a semi up to Boston and back in the winter months. At least the oil truck had come a few days ago, Ida went on, so it should stay warm enough. Did she need anything, she had asked, well good then, she'd be by when she could be. "Sorry the telephone ain't working," she added, an afterthought. "The service was cut off long ago. Used to be a phone up at the packing shed, if you need to use one." Ida thought *that* was still working. Was, last she'd checked. "You a little bit, girlie," she said, eyeing last week's largely untouched box of canned goods. Something flickered

in her eyes. "Next time I come I'm bringing you some of my pepper pot soup. Nice veal tripe. Dumplings. Do you good."

Silas's letters were pages and pages long, the diction inflated, the script almost unreadable, paranoid, the way he could be. The mafia owns Teaneck. Well, Marlise thought that was probably true. Lately, renewed rants about Nixon, war conspiracies, Kent State, a newly arrived, tripped-out hall-mate attempting to smother him with a pillow at night. He described a ward field trip to the Zoo, where he had leapt over a cement barricade and climbed the bars of the gorilla cage, screaming for release of the primates. They'd pulled him down, his pants sodden with urine. Now his parents and doctors were talking in earnest and with some urgency about electro-convulsive therapy, trying another, less permissive hospital, even though Silas was twenty and would soon be considered an adult. "I miss the circuitry of your sweet ears, my lady," he'd written in his strange mix of capital and small letters, some cursive mixed in among the printing. He'd put an oblong lasso of asterisks around this statement.

She had let him. First licking the lobes, then the whorled crescents, finally taking each ear entirely into his mouth. This was about as far as anything sexual had gone on between Marlise and Silas until that chocolate kiss on her inner thigh, but his doing this thing with her ears made her come close to having what she thought might be an orgasm. She was, she believed, still a virgin; there was so much she didn't know, or know how or whom to ask. And why was she crying now, suddenly, she, Marlise Schade, who never cried?

Silas's missives exhausted Marlise, though she thought she should try to read every word of them, in case, embedded in the illegible thicket of prose, was something, even an inkling,

about Silas trying to kill himself again. Not that she now had any way of letting anybody know if he were planning such a thing. Well, she had Dr. Lance's telephone numbers, office and home, on a card in her suitcase. "I do hope you will call me at any time, for any reason," he had said at their last session. Was there really a telephone anywhere about this place? And would she remember how to talk if she could find one?

How to help Silas? How to reach him? She'd found it impossible to finish any one of the letters she started to him, though she knew that Windy Bill would see they got posted if she sent them off with Ida. Marlise was tired. As the boxes from Ida came, she felt less and less inclined to open cans, heat soup, nibble crackers or cereal. At first, with no one watching, monitoring, like those unsupervised weeks at Barton, she'd felt newly exhilarated. She ran through the rooms, sprinted up and down the stairs. Danced and sang in the dark. Took long hot baths, fed the birds and cats. But now, with these letters intruding and the hours looming large around her, she was stalled. And the longer she put off reading, writing, eating, the flatter and duller she felt.

Once, back at The Institute, pinching her thin forearm, downy with hair, Silas had held the speck of flesh between his fingers for a bit, then put those two fingers to his lips. She was afraid then that he might say something about her condition, but he didn't. He never had, never did, and seemed, unbelievably, to find her lovely. "I see you in all your ages," he had said, adding "Child. Daughter. Mother."

She had just come back from a session with Dr. Lance. Much of that hour had been spent, as usual, in silence. Marlise did appreciate that Dr. L, unlike others, didn't make her talk or try to fill the silence by talking himself. Occasionally he

would ask her questions about her relationship with Maurice or with the boys at Barton, or suggest that not eating to the point of almost disappearing might be a way of avoiding sexual encounters. Usually she didn't respond to these kinds of questions, but sometimes she'd make things up. "Oh, well. If you must know, I did french-kiss a girl at school," she'd said aloud that very afternoon, her own voice strange to her among the drapes and framed diplomas. "Does that count? It was just the one time." A pause. She didn't even really know what a "french" kiss was. "Did you enjoy it," Lancelot asked. "No," she'd said, "but I find *you* very attractive."

Who was she when she said such banal and stupid things? Dr. Lance peered at his notepad in the office gloam, inscrutable as always, his fountain pen quietly scratching. "That's the problem with these people," Silas always said. "Dyed-in-the-wool Freudians. They think it all always boils down to daddy and mommy." He continued stroking her arm. "But for you, it's sex, right? Not your parents' sex, not sex with your parents, not sex with anyone else, but yours? Your own sex. Sexiness. You're afraid of your body and what it can hold and feel. It's okay. Bodies are scary. I don't mean *having sex*, either. I mean *being* sexual. In everything you do and are. The way you think. That's what I think."

Marlise didn't know what this meant or what to say to him when he said things like that. What she said now, sitting in the hallway with Silas after her session, was repeat back to him what he had said to her. "You see me. A child. A daughter, mother." She swallowed. "Not wife?"

Immediately she knew how hopeless and old-fashioned that sounded. Silas looked down. "No," he finally said. "Not that." Then, "Lover. Lover maybe."

Marlise's heart pounded. It had been a moment for them. A terrible risk, looking like that into their future, as if they might have one, together. Or with anyone else. Or at all.

"Have a cookie?" Dr. Lance would always say at the end of each hour, pulling a tin of small round Swedish gingersnaps from a drawer.

"Sure," she'd say, taking a fistful and stuffing them into the pockets of her baggy painter's pants, already crumbly with the ones she'd accepted last time. Later she'd scatter them for the starlings she passed along the paths of the fenced-in courtyard.

"Here," she'd said to Silas, her arm still pink where he had held her skin, her fingers still at his lips as though he were slowly eating her. "Have a cookie." She pulled some ginger crumbs out of a pocket.

"You think I'm one of your birds," he'd said, putting her palm to his mouth, pecking at the bits, then licking it noisily clean, tongue lingering between each finger.

What about you, she wanted to ask Silas, who was putting her now wet hand to his mouth. Will you . . . will we. . . . ?

She didn't say this aloud. She knew they were giving him big doses of something for the mania with which he'd catapulted into her life in September. For his paranoia. His sadness. His suicidal thoughts. Sometimes his hands shook violently after one of his own sessions with Dr. Everdeen, The Institute's head shrink. On the other hand, Silas seemed to still have special status on the ward—bumming cigarettes from the nurses, though patient smoking was strictly forbidden, joking with the aides, milling among the patients with a warm word for everyone, keeping them all tethered, but also at a distance, Marlise at his side. He had, Marlise realized, the

dubious privilege of being, at twenty, already something like a lifer.

"Tell me something about you," she'd said instead.

He kissed her hand and returned it to her lap. "Ha-ha, really? Well, okay, Dr. Schade, they tell me I tried to stuff my baby sister between the wall and my parents' bed after they brought her home from hospital. I also peed on her a couple of times."

Marlise laughed. "No, really," he said. "I did that. I peed a lot. I did it at the library once. I tried to ask to use the toilet, but my accent wasn't good enough and the Swiss librarian didn't understand my English. So I took a whiz back in the stacks."

"I hope you watered something good," she said, smiling.

"Oh, it was. It was Novalis," he said, suddenly brightening. "So much for the Enlightenment, right? Have you ever had a pickled goose egg? Used a chamber pot? But, since you asked, Fraulein Doktor: back to my sister. She's just now eighteen, but already manager of a swanky art gallery in Paris. I'm pretty sure she slept with a great many important people to get that gig."

Was Silas a liar? Marlise wondered. How had he known about Novalis when he was just a little boy? Maybe he hadn't actually been that little. Marlise had heard him say other things she wasn't sure were true. "I'm just putting in some vacation time here," he'd boasted once, early on, to a cluster of disciples seated on the floor around him. "Until I'm twenty-one. Then I'm out of this place and all places like it. Out for good. There are at least three New York galleries just waiting for my new work!"

"So you'll leave me," she had said, later.

"Never," he'd said, brushing an eyelash from her cheek and then putting it on his tongue. He grinned, winked, and swallowed. She had believed him. But then, unexpectedly, after all, it had been she, Marlise, who had had to leave—the bankrupt trust fund, the precipitous news from Maurice, the lunch at La Terrasse, the bus ride to New Jersey, the Rancocas, the Close, the lonely old house with a dead tree at its abandoned heart. And now these letters reaching her, each one wilder and more difficult to fathom than the last.

The Close, Summer 1940s

All in all, just under two hundred acres, and as a girl, Beatrice Schade, Bea, had roamed the farm freely, especially in summer when school let out. In corn season, huge wings of irrigated water pumped in from the river wheeled over a sea of tassels, the heavy horses, heads festooned with oak-leaf sprays to keep off the flies, ready at the market wagons in the yard, men with blades and balsa baskets for packing. Later, trucks for all this. A tractor. Harrows. Tin cup on a chain at the trough, the water icy and tasting of scallions. Then the peaches coming on in full August attar, the packing shed a din, men's voices rising over the hulking green Niagara sorter, its felted chutes and rollers churning all day, even into some evenings, the imperfect fruit, stones and all, flung into crimson carnage through open back doors, scarves of bees thrumming there. Ladders leaning into tossing bladed tops of trees, rows and rows of them. Men's voices from these treetops. Italians from Philadelphia and elsewhere, who came on trucks each day, seasonally, to help with the picking. A whistle coming from them sometimes as she passed, on through the fields and orchards smelling of ginger, the soil so fine they called it "sugar sand."

Along the river was how she usually went, past the smokehouse, out-house privy (bags of fertilizer stored in there by then), the apple copse with its hives of bees and waxy screens of honey, dog pen, houses on stilts, some with skiffs or rafts

tied up outside, strung-up trousers of the squatters who'd come in off the rails before, during, and after the Depression, mostly men, all named Bill, it seemed to Beatrice, Windy Bill, Bad Bill, Pleasant Bill, and Bill Elmer, whose shack had caught on fire, dying when the drifter went back in for something valuable, the extensive acreage of Paradise Close bristling with such shacks and lean-tos, where hobos and travelers came and went over the decades, especially during hard times, thanks to the leniency or indifference of the Schades.

To get to Ida's, Bea had to pass through a dark patch of woods on a rough lane everyone called "the little bridge," grateful for the cool cover of tall oaks, locusts, maples. If she squinted, she could see into and beyond them to the golden slopes of the small vineyard, her grandfather's passion and his folly, gone mostly fallow later, during Prohibition, though the canes and wires were still tangled with vines. The woodsy path was fragrant, edged with fox grape and the honeysuckle trumpets she plucked and nipped at the tips to sip the nectar.

As a child, Bea spent hours with Ida while Ida's husband, Brut, who kept a little marina—mostly men from Philadelphia coming over to fish and cool off in the summer, or to go gunning for small game in the winter—worked and loafed outside. Ida served the men meals and sometimes a little rye whiskey ("Your grandfather tried to get me to serve his wine when he was still alive," Ida once said to Bea. "Know why not? Vinegar is why not"). And while Ida stewed tomatoes or gutted fish, fried eels (all jittery in the pan, even dead and skinned), jiggled clams open with a quick, sharp blade, Bea would wander out among chicken-wire pens of animals, a kind of sanctuary back there. A box turtle, round as a sapling and missing a foot, that Ida said was older than Bea's

father and would likely outlive even Beatrice and any children she might have. Always a succession of injured hawks. Once a flying squirrel that swung freely about the kitchen, curtains to wire-dropped light bulb to doorjamb. A fox was kept in its own pen, far from the chickens. A series of owls. Sometimes Ida let Bea make the chicken mash—clam and oyster shells thrown into a grinder with field-corn cobs—silky in her hands, the hens flocking at her feet in a cobble of pecks and nerves.

On inclement or overcast days, Ida, a young wife then, though she had no children of her own, would sit and talk, making observations about the men who visited the marina or offering bits of news about the Bills and some of the other people, like herself and Brut, who lived on or about the Close—Olive Brick from up the crick, who had just been diagnosed with the cancer, like Beatrice's father, or the old German umbrella-maker and his nephew Otto (both confirmed bachelors, she winked, though Beatrice failed to understand), who shared a cabin up beyond the vineyard.

"Who buys them from them," Beatrice had asked. "The umbrellas." Beatrice had an umbrella that she carried on rainy days, but she was quite sure it came from Strawbridge & Clothier or John Wanamaker's. "Can't say," said Ida. "Mostly it's got to be just repairs they do now, I guess. Anybody wants one can get an umbrella at a store." Ida said it that way, "umberella." "I guess some people are more thrifty than others, want to keep the old ones going. Me and Brut wear oil coats in the rain. Got hoods on them, you see. Keeps hands free. Got no need for a umberella."

Bea's favorite was the story Ida told about how one afternoon Bea's grandfather was walking the property when he

came upon the poet Walt Whitman, naked as a baby, sitting up to his neck in the Rancocas among the splatter-docks, rubbing himself down with clay-like mud from the creek bottom and slapping his shoulders with a willow switch. "Are you *sure* it was *Walt Whitman*?" Bea asked Ida. By then she knew of the poet and had even recited, standing beside her desk in her grade school classroom, "O Captain, My Captain." "Oh, sure, sure as you're born it was him, your grandfather knew of him from some farm people down at Laurel Springs," Ida said. "White Horse, they called it then. The old poet had been sick and sometimes came on from Camden to stay at the Laurel Springs place, set along a crick, Timber, I believe it was, but he came on up this way one day, running an errand with some boy in a wagon, and took a notion to swim since the afternoon was warmish. Your grandfather himself stripped down and took a bath too, and then sent the poet and his wagon friend off back to Laurel Springs with some bottles of his terrible wine."

The Close, March 1971

Some things you know before you can possibly know them. Other things persist in their mysteries, untranslatable: wet latch of rain pelting a red silk parasol, but not the rain itself, not the sky that shed them. Leaves, forests, birds, clock-cases, ribs splayed under a fine, sun-struck skin. Bodies are not figments, are not time, split and fusing atoms, desire in fugue state, the stars in their courses. Secrets within, like another person. Savage, grief offers two paths, one back to waking, the other deeper into the dream. If we step toward waking, do we stop dreaming, afraid of what the dream might see? A hunger so implacable we might put out a hand and touch it. Not everything can speak what it suffers.

When Otto Wenner got to thinking this way, he wondered if his winter woolgathering was a sign of late life rejuvenation or of impending death—the fact, at seventy-one, of his eight-decades-old cells dying out and spreading dread through him, as it did when he woke, repeatedly, at night, his heart jolting. Just the evening before, he'd dreamed of his Uncle Augustus's candy shop in a Philadelphia brownstone. He'd been in the whitewashed cellar among the copper pots and burners, the nineteenth-century molds for making clear sugar glass animals—amber horses, claret elephants, ducklings green as emeralds. He was inside a sugar egg, the kind some called "enchanted," looking toward a ship's porthole rimmed with green leaves made of icing, like a laurel wreath.

What lay beyond made his chest thump, a large hand reaching inside, and Otto had awakened in his dark room, speaking German. He shook himself now, eyes glancing toward his work-bench, where his large hands often moved, freckled and antique among the scattered worm-springs, slip rivets, sheets of oiled Japanese paper. Glue pots and brushes. Wood-carving knives. Dusty bolts of moth-eaten umbrella silks. The window had darkened to the blue of coming snow.

Otto stepped outside onto the porch of his little cabin on the property of Paradise Close. Fresh air, he thought, might help loosen his constricted chest. Behind him, back inside the house and workshop, through the static of a Philadelphia radio station, someone was talking about a coming snow storm. Otto stepped down from the porch, rounded a corner of the cabin, and fetched a sturdy shovel from a lean-to set against the north wall. Best to have a shovel inside the house, should the snow be bad. Not that he felt much like shoveling snow these days, his chest heavy, his ankles swollen.

Otto stood with the shovel on the porch. The impending blizzard got his mind meandering again, again back to his boyhood in Philadelphia, and of how, when his mother had at last been able to cross the sea to America to join him, she had been detained in a place along the Delaware with other immigrants who were sick. And so as often as he could he would leave his uncle's bakery, where he worked, and run all the long way across the city, down to the wharves, where in a large building they held the passengers who were too infectious to move into the streets and houses with their families. He'd look up at the way-station, guessing which window might be hers. If she looked out, was well enough to stand up and do so, maybe she would see him, and know how much he

missed and loved her, though he hoped, too, that she would not know that he sometimes could not remember her face. He recalled her smell, though: goat milk, oats, soap. Dumplings. Potato peelings, her wrists sunk in a bucket of silky water.

And would she recognize him, grown so much taller these past two years since he'd come over with his uncles and their families? She had stayed behind in Germany to nurse his dying father, who was now buried across the sea, never to be seen by Otto, or anyone, again.

Most mornings as a boy in Philadelphia he'd worked at the bakery of his dead father's brother Fritz, hauling burlap and linen sacks of flour and sugar from wagons down into the cellar, catching rats, sweeping, running things up and down the stairs. Uncle Fritz did the baking—breads, rolls, cheese-cakes—in the cellar at night, and Otto slept there on a kip in the sugary warmth of dough and ovens. It was Fritz's wife and daughters who ran the shop at street level by day. In the afternoons, Otto would work with another uncle, Harald, his mother's brother, who was employed by an umbrella maker and purveyor. The owner kept a fancy shop, but Harald would go from door to door on his behalf, repairing umbrellas on doorsteps, around to the backs of businesses, on the street, at the gentlemen's clubs, anywhere around the city. The boy Otto helped to carry the tools in a cupboard strapped to his back, bristling inside with the necessary ribs and tips and patching cloths. A paper of needles. Spools of thick thread. Cloth. Shears. Those were the days when people held on to things, didn't throw them out for a new one, Otto thought. And a thing was hand-made, and made well.

Eventually, when the umbrella shop owner passed away, Uncle Harald inherited all of the deceased man's inventory

and tools. The markets had crashed by then, and Otto left the city, moving with Uncle Harald to a property across the Delaware in southern New Jersey, up along Rancocas Creek, to this very cabin, where they'd set up a small shop and household on a farm owned by the Schade family, originally German people also, and known for taking in strays. Otto was himself a young man by then, in his twenties, but because he and his uncle rarely spoke to one another, he never fully understood the reason for the move to this particular spot, which seemed, to the younger man, as remote as the moon.

Almost unbelievably, though, Harald had kept many of his city customers, one in particular, a high-end clothier, who came loyally once a month despite the Depression with a wagon to fetch specially commissioned items to take back, fine silk parasols for ladies, elegant lampshades, over-sized brollies for golfers. Some with hand-carved handles—an ivory swan's head and neck, fine-turned, burled maple. Some, Otto realized early on, shaped like phalluses. Others cleft like a woman's parts. Quite a market for these, actually, judging from the orders, Harald doing the carving at the workbench by hand, quietly, deliberately, Otto helping out with repairs, keeping the books. People somehow found the place. Fewer and fewer came, though, as the years passed, until finally business trickled to a stop, and customers no longer made their way to the cottage in the woods of Paradise Close, to have their old umbrellas and lamp shades repaired or to buy a new one.

It had been winter on the one day in particular that Otto was remembering from his boyhood, months after the last boat from Bavaria had come up the Delaware that year. That afternoon, the river was frozen up in big blocks and chops,

and he'd run out onto the ice, slipping, no gloves or mittens, his breath trailing behind him, and he recalled hearing in the school he sometimes attended about how General George Washington, the first American president, had braved the ice of this very river to cross over into Trenton Town and win a battle against the surprised and drunken Hessians. That story made him wince. Hessians, some boys said, were Germans, and Otto would go silent then, hoping not to be noticed. He much preferred to learn what he could from reading the piles of books his Aunt Louisa, Uncle Fritz's wife, who had been trained as a teacher in Bamberg, brought home from the lending library: Goethe, Tolstoy, Alger, German and English editions of Dickens, Melville, Stevenson. The many newspapers.

That cold day he'd clambered out over the floes, reckless, free, he was a pirate from one of these stories, on the bounding main, clenching an invisible dagger in his teeth, the skeletal winter copses of New Jersey on the far shore transformed into a flotilla of ships approaching, until a man on the city side of the river walked out to the dock's edge, waving his cap, his arms, and shouting at him, his adult voice thin in the frozen air, calling him back off the ice, over to shore.

Otto had expected to be scolded when he scrambled up onto the pier, his fists blue and numb when he shoved them into shallow pockets, eyes cast down. But then a voice from above and a hand on his shoulder, firm, fatherly, was relaying the news that his mother—"Frau Wenner, yes, ja?"—had died earlier that very week, not of typhoid, as it turned out, but of peritonitis, sadly, and he, this gentleman, a doctor he was, or maybe a priest, though he wore no collar, was truly sorry to have to impart the news to him this way; he had

been just preparing to write to the uncles. He had seen Otto waiting outside on many days, even in the rain, and Otto must become a little man himself now, because his parents were both dead, and he was old enough and deserved to be told the truth.

Peritonitis. It was a word unknown to Otto that day, but one whose syllables he'd repeat and then later learned all too well. By the time he reached adulthood he'd known six family members, adults and children, uncles, aunts, cousins, to die from it, swiftly, often overnight or in the course of a single day. The word filled him with a particular grief, a sense of disbelief, bad luck, shame, and waste.

But that was years, years ago. Now, from the porch of a small cabin on the property of the Close, as a black cat wreathed his stiff blue ankles, old Otto watched the first icy flecks of incoming storm materialize among the fallen vine trellises of the far field with the subtle threat of a migraine aura. The sky toward the river, hidden behind hedges thick with pheasants, rabbits, appeared to stir like fabric and concussed a moment. Could that be thunder? Thunder in a snowstorm? Another smothered pock like gunshot, then a staccato tick of ice pellets on the tin roof above. His thoughts turned to Ida, still at the marina and to Windy Bill, alive out in his shack over the creek, as far as Otto knew. Remnants, all of them, himself included, of times long past. Who would be out with a gun in this weather? Otto wondered, closing the door and locking it, as if to shut out the alarm, the storm, the racket inside him.

The Close, June 1955

All morning Beatrice felt as though she were being dreamed by someone else. "There came a day at summer's full, entirely for me," she thought, stepping out onto the wide gray boards of the front porch of the big house, coffee cup in hand, remembering some lines from her favorite poet, Miss Emily Dickinson. Or for you, she thought. You, Dreamer, wherever, whoever, you are.

The Rancocas silvered with June heat. Around her lay the quiet Close, caught in a spell of stasis. Or was it stirring? Just two days before, Beatrice and her husband Blue and her older brother Cole and a few friends and distant relations—the Ebles, Bea's childhood friend Maurice, who'd grown up on a neighboring property, and Maurice's two young sons and new bride—had buried her mother across the river in the Riverside Lutheran church-yard, beside her father and his parents, in the plot her great-grandfather had bought for the Schade family in a previous century. Two unused plots remained, thick with matted grass beneath a brilliant brocade of elm shadow—for herself and her brother Cole, she guessed, the last of the Schades her ancestor had accounted for, though probably Beatrice would at some future time lie with Blue and the other Wells clan, now that she was married and living closer to them, and despite the fact—to the barely disguised disapproval of Blue's folks—that she'd not given up her own surname. Cole lived in Virginia; that's how Bea had

met Blue, she in school there at a small women's college close by the University where her brother and Blue had belonged to the same fraternity and gone to law school.

Cole had pushed off right after the funeral lunch that Bea had arranged at the Close, crab salad sandwiches and champagne, Cole, already drunk by noon, chain-smoking and never one much for people in recent years, mumbling about his real estate dealings in the south and making promises to Bea and Blue that he'd help see to the Land Use permit, to finding tenants maybe, and other legalities for the Close. Putting his degree to use. This very morning, while she'd pretended to sleep, Blue had risen before dawn to ride with Brut and catch a train back to New York, where work on a particularly thorny entertainment property case of some sort had kept him away from their home in a Maryland suburb for most of this past year, the first year of their marriage.

Beatrice hadn't minded. She'd liked being alone in their small ranch house, was used to solitude, didn't easily make or particularly need friends, and lived near enough to take a bus into the District to visit the monuments, the museums and stores, whenever she wanted to. And the Maryland suburbs also put her a couple hundred miles away from her mother, with whom Bea had never been close and who had lost her mind to dementia. She hadn't even known who Beatrice was on her wedding day. Still, Beatrice had wanted the ceremony held at the Close, on the front lawn, under the plane trees, her mother in a wheelchair, looked in upon daily by Ida and attended by the two nurses, women from Delanco, who had taken turns caring for her in the house for many years, and who—although she, the elder Mrs. Schade, had long ago forgotten that she had been an alcoholic—still enjoyed having

a glass of bourbon and ginger passed beneath her nose every evening before supper.

For the first time, perhaps ever, Beatrice Schade was completely alone in the old house where she'd been raised until she was sent away to school. Though she loved the house, admired its strangeness—that old pear tree, rooted in the deeps of the earth and shooting right up the middle of it, the rotting casks of wine in the cellars, the sheds with their stench of yeast and haymow—she also never felt that the place had wanted her in return. Free of parents at last, free—for a while—of her husband, Bea felt the ancient tree trunk in the house behind her and the musky river and the sweet corn-silk heat before her seep into her, dilating the world she'd always felt had never been hungry enough to love her back.

On that morning after her mother's funeral, alone on the Close, grown-up Bea, married Bea, set forth. It was her girlhood path she took, the morning charmed around her, in the wake of her fresh losses and in a full flush of freedom and longing she had not anticipated and could not explain. But when she got to the scrap of woods that led to Ida and Brut's, instead of taking the path to the marina, she veered off into the understory, in the direction of the vineyard. Sweating, holding up her dress hem, and swatting gnats and flies off her bare legs, she skirted the slope, many of the vineyard's double-curtain and single trellises long fallen, but some of the vines and spurs still quick and spiraling, a few nodes, green clusters of fruit here and there. Insects. A motorboat snarling on the river. Up a small rise she went, across a thicket of bay and locust trees, the privet hedges a trench of camphor, and into a clearing.

Otto was standing outside the small house, as though waiting for her.

"It's you."

"Yes. I came—"

"Your mother. I heard. I am sorry."

His voice was rusty, perhaps from little use or something caught in his throat, and he must by now be somewhere in his fifties, but his eyes were still kind, an icy blue-gray, like the eyes of a wolf Beatrice had seen once penned in a zoo.

"I actually came to see—," she began.

"It's still here, look."

Otto bent to unlatch and lift the painted slatting beneath his porch and withdrew a plank of wood, perhaps an old cupboard door or shutter, and on top of it something about the size of a bushel basket draped beneath a piece of oil cloth.

He placed this board on the porch. Beatrice stepped closer as he lifted the oiled fabric with a tenderness his large scarred hands belied. And there it was, the grapevine and sapling-wattled doll's house she had fashioned the summer she'd turned ten, its jumble of twigs and leaves and twine now blowsy, mouse-nested, but mostly intact.

That was the summer she'd been left almost entirely alone, turned nearly feral, those last three months of her father's final illness, and she'd ranged through parts of the Close that were unknown even to her, squatting to pee and shit in the woods, eating raw corn from the cob, teeth full of silk, devouring peaches she picked up off the ground or tugged down from the trees, sometimes without hands, like a deer, her mouth sticky, stained with fruit stones, grape-skins, and soil.

She'd started building the doll house when she'd come upon a large felled tree, its roots dendritic, the trunk hollow.

She'd peered inside, brushing aside a thick spider web that stuck to one side like a theater curtain. After that it had been something to do, to gather sticks, truss them up with grapevine and later with string from home, making walls with strips of bark, lining the floors with carefully transferred mosses. A house in a tree, she'd thought to herself. Like a tree in a house.

She'd begun it there, in the mouth of the felled tree at first, but when her little house got too big for that space, she'd carefully moved the construction to one side of the fallen trunk. After a spell of heavy storms, though, that kept her indoors, she'd returned to the woods to find her fairy house mostly demolished, so she began re-building, more ambitiously, adding rooms, a lean-to. Clothespins pocketed from Ida's became a family. Two wine corks from the cellar and stuck with toothpicks were corgis, like those that attended the young English princess. Then one day, about a week after her father's death, during which time she'd been away from the woods, she arrived to find erected over her little house a sturdy pavilion, constructed of 20-inch high polished bamboo stilts holding up an elaborately folded coral, skirted tent of pleated, waxed fabric, beaded with dew.

Now Otto was saying, "Come inside, Beatrice, if you want, I've still got the rest of it."

There, in Otto's dark front room that was also the workroom, on a side table, was the orange paper pavilion.

"And you still have them," she said, "the little umbrellas you made for the family!" They were lined up on a shelf, miniature like the ones in exotic cocktails, but made of saffron and rose silks and bamboo toothpicks.

"That's when I first saw you," she said. "Well, first I saw your feet. Shoes, I mean." She smiled at him. "I'd climbed up

through the woods after Father died, and was kneeling beside my little house, marveling at its tent that seemed to have dropped like Aladdin's carpet from the sky. Then those two old shoes beside me and you, standing there above me, both hands bristling with little fairy umbrellas. It was so—charming. I wasn't the least afraid."

"No."

The magic of Otto's place steeped back into her. The ceiling low and hung with oriental parasols, upside down, like lanterns. Shelves of flat luxurious papers, bundles of bone, bamboo, and metal ribs, wood carving tools, brown glass jars of long-congealed mastic, huge shears fit for the large hands of men like Otto's now dead uncle Harald, who was still alive back then but spoke little English and sat quietly, a corner cipher in a blue smock, and of Otto himself, kindly maker of fanciful toys for a lonely child, the worktable always pushed under the window. A cat watched from the windowsill. The cuckoo clock, still broken, hands fixed at 3:30, still hung beside the door to the small bedroom, its carved leaves and iron pine-cone pendulums motionless and calm.

"Now you are married."

"Yes."

"You left after that summer."

"After Father died. To school. Mother sent me. Then off to college, you know. Down South. Do you know, every Friday for a long, long time I remembered that you sometimes called me 'Friday.' I'd said to you, 'because I visit you on Fridays?' And you said no, like 'Friday,' in the book about the shipwrecked man. You confused me because I came almost every day that summer to see you and the fairy house, not just Fridays."

"Ja. Yes."

"'I so earnestly longed for somebody to speak to.' That is what you said."

"Did I. Like that, exactly?" Otto smiled at her.

"I was only ten then. Now I'm 21. I've read the book."

"Have you, then."

"I have," she said.

Then Bea knelt, arranging the full circle of her skirt in a fan on the floor as she did so. She took her time. Otto didn't move. Slowly, with hands trembling but also deliberate, she properly unfolded and then folded up again the hems of each of his trouser legs. Lint in there. Grass. Colored thread. Twigs. She brushed this out first. Two folds back up. She untied the laces of his old-fashioned leather shoes. He let her pull them off, holding his ankles as she did so. Then the socks, woolen even in this weather. She lowered her mouth to the tender oyster of flesh that floats above the sole and just beneath the inner ankle bone. First the right foot, then the left, with all of the long-pent gratitude for being so long ago seen and cared for that she could muster.

*

Blue's business kept him away in the city, and Bea stayed on at the Close. Blue was, truth be told, still a stranger to Bea. Handsome, urbane, savvy with money, he had seemed to want to marry her to complete some sort of picture he had of himself, of what his, what their life should be. She'd been drawn along into it, not wanting to return home after school, not sure what her degree in English Literature would allow her to do anyway. Blue had been a friend of her brother Cole, and it had all just sort of happened. Marrying Blue had felt

like the safe, the inevitable course, and since by this time he was traveling many days out of every month, that year of conjugal life had been bearable.

It was by now mid-July and the old bottling shed was warm with winey heat and a faint, sweet trace of horse stalls. Otto and Beatrice pushed closed the big door, large enough to let a flat truck or tractor through, but Otto had opened a window, little more than a square cut into the wall that swung into the room and closed with a wooden peg, up in the loft where they'd made a pallet of quilts. In the gloom below them, the old winepress that Bea, when she was a girl, thought looked like a giant wooden screw, stood, totemic, with outstretched arms. Shelves of barrels. Vinegar-bitten oak casks. Dust-grimed empties. A few drunk flies.

Bea lay on her stomach examining a pile of books Otto had brought for her. "I've read this one," she said, pointing lazily toward a spine lettered with *Far From the Madding Crowd*. She pulled another from the stack, Gothic lettering on the worn paper cover. "*Das Stundenbuch . . . ,*" she began, trying out her German. Behind her Otto was pushing up her dress, gently tugging down what was beneath. "Wait," she said, pointing to the damp, rust-red string between her legs. "Started this morning," she said. He shook his head. "This may hurt," he said, "I'm sorry Beatrice." He always called her by her full name. "Beatrice," he said again, pronouncing each syllable, licking a thumb to find another way, exploding almost before he was inside her. And, true, it *had* hurt. But it had also been so enthralling for them both that they made love again this way again twice more before the loft began to turn gold, and evening stepped in fully to claim the summer day.

Philadelphia, Early spring 1914

The boy Otto had been down to the river most of the afternoon looking at the ships, but had returned to the umbrella shop where Uncle Harald wasn't expected back for an hour or more. With a little daylight left, Harald would still be out doing umbrella repairs about town on his own, having given the boy permission to rove a bit. Harald was, Otto knew, different. "Slow" was what Aunt Louisa called him. Which was why the family was grateful that he'd found work with the umbrella maker and that Otto, such a bright boy, was able to help him when he went out on his repair rounds, explain things, keep the money right, if Harald got confused. So Otto had been reluctant to leave him on his own that day, but was also grateful for the reprieve. The river, ships, barges loaded and going places, had made him lonesome, though, which is why he'd come back early.

Otto went around to the back of the shop, to a back door into the English basement, which opened into a storage area and which was also where Harald lived: small cot, chair, a sink. Canned goods in a metal standing closet. Small camp stove. Otto had not called out to announce his return to Uncle Harald since Otto had expected the place to be empty.

It was shadowy, late afternoon, but some noise came from the corner. Rats, Otto thought. Then breathing, bigger animal sounds. Grunts. His eyes adjusted, but what was he seeing? Two bodies, one bent, one standing behind the other

and both of them rocking, rocking. Slapping sounds. Otto was mesmerized. But he stepped back, shutting the door as quietly as he could. He was blocks away before he acknowledged two things. The standing figure was the shop-owner, his shirt unbuttoned, a jewel pinned in his necktie glinting in the dark. But also: the doe eyes of Uncle Harald, on hands and knees, opening to meet Otto's. So much in that look, Otto thought, yet so much hidden in it too. What Otto knew then was that on his dead mother's behalf he must never abandon her brother Harald, that whatever secrets his uncle had were not bad ones or good ones, but that Harald by himself could not protect them.

The Close, August 1955

It would not be an exaggeration to say that they seemed to fuck continually and in every possible way they could imagine, in the woods, the old vineyard, in tall grasses beside the river, in the house, in bathtubs, in sheds, in the barn. Or backed up against the old tree trunk on the second-floor landing, like Eve and Adam. Otto rolling her onto her side, or his hot breath and tongue at all her openings, the quilt, grasses, his body gripped in her fists. Beatrice astride his mouth or his torso, facing his face, facing his feet, falling toward them afterwards, streaming with sweat.

In the evenings, when Otto returned to his little house—why?, to preserve some old-fashioned sense of order, maybe, or protocol, an acknowledgment of her married state or of his own, long-solitary existence?—Beatrice would pull bits of straw or grass from her body, put her own fingers where his had been to extract the smell of him. Or she'd cup a hand to her lips, breathe in the oceanic spindrift of cock, of semen bringing her to yet another orgasm, alone there, restless on the prim, corded spread of the bed where she'd slept as a girl. And surely that was part of it, the coming, orgasm, climaxing, silly names for the terrifying pleasure of it, all new to her. She did not know about Otto, and of course he was older and certainly seemed experienced, but he also struck her as being in a perpetual state of surprise, arousal, and gratitude as well.

Afterwards they would eat, Otto scrambling eggs Beatrice had fetched from Ida's, beaten and browned in butter with summer onions. Cold bottles of Alsatian wine Otto purchased from a market in Riverside. Little grilled sausages with wild cherry tomatoes foraged from abandoned garden beds about the Close. Later, Bea wondered at the purity of their appetites and why they hadn't been stalked by desperation, by the looming constraints of their contracted time together. Where had that trust come from? Those early days with the little toy house in the woods? The pavilion and umbrellas that had seemed as protective, veiled, and yet transparent as the light of allayed loneliness that suffused them?

One afternoon in early August, Beatrice took some photos of Otto, naked in the wine shed loft, with her camera. His risen cock as he stood before her made him vulnerable in a way that convulsed her with what she was beginning to realize was love. Love at last. He had insisted on taking a photo of her, too, after she'd gotten dressed, holding over her shoulder the crimson damasked parasol he'd made for her to match the lampshade he'd fashioned for the floor lamp she read by at night, up at her family's house, when they parted ways at night, she with books he gave to her, he with beautiful large, empty hands swinging by his sides as he made his way back to the cabin.

But the afternoon late that month when Blue phoned to say that he was done for now with his business in New York and would be collecting her for the return trip south the following day, Bea put the heavy receiver back in its cradle. She sat at the small telephone table for a while, then slipped on her shoes and ran all the way along the river and up through

the vineyard to Otto's cabin. She was weeping but tried to speak.

Otto put his fingers to her lips. What happened next, there beneath the ceiling hung with exotic parasols, the thongs of silk wrapping ankles and wrists to table legs, strips of soft cloth blindfolding their eyes, the endless yards of unbolted fabric with which they swaddled and bound and unbandaged one another, happened all night, and without one word.

*

Within weeks of her return south, Beatrice knew she was pregnant. What to do? Her impulse was to take the next bus north, to find Otto, to tell him, to leave Blue. But would Otto... want this? So much older, set in his ways. And how to leave Blue, friend of her brother, earner of their income, and just preoccupied enough to leave Beatrice to her own solitary ways? Perhaps she was mistaken. She waited.

When she could no longer hide the fact from herself, she told Blue. And because they'd rarely had sex—certainly none in those summer months when she was at the Close and he in New York, but also before that, ever since they'd married, not because they hadn't, at first, attempted, but because things had never quite worked, Blue always on top and often going limp and then sulking, and because of what had come to be, eventually, a not intolerable indifference on both sides; and because Beatrice had not known how to talk about the impotence, the pregnancy, or if she even should speak of it, because of all of this, Blue surmised her unfaithfulness, though she would never say with whom. Blue suspected Maurice, her childhood friend who, despite

having been married a couple of times already, had always been, like everyone, it seemed, always in love with Beatrice Schade.

And so to hurt her back, and because it was true and had been weighing on him, he confessed what she'd already half-guessed: that he really loved men, not women, and in fact had had many lovers, including, once, he lied, drunk at Sigma Nu, her brother Cole, and that there was, and this was no lie, someone in New York, as well, more than one someone, actually, which was the real reason for his frequent and protracted trips away.

Ironically, though, Blue, for the remaining months of Beatrice's pregnancy, gave up his relentless traveling away and took to staying close to home. He rarely left their ranch house on the cul de sac outside of Washington, even to run an errand, conducting his business mostly by telephone and mail. He seldom left her alone for any reason, going so far as to accompany her to the grocery store. The A&P, for goodness sake, where Beatrice had never once before known him to darken the door. He hid the car keys from her, and leapt to answer the telephone whenever it rang. He is terrified, she thought. Territorial, panicked, and furious in a way that stripped away all the artifice of the marriage that at the same time she must now take painful steps to preserve for the sake of her coming child.

These things they told no one. The Wellses had been pleased—an heir. Otto had no telephone, and although Beatrice started several letters to him, she never sent them. It occurred to her that she'd not given Otto any way to reach her—no address, no number. In a hedge at the far edge of the property, she burned her unsent letters, along with the

photographs and negatives she had taken of him in the wine loft, developing the roll of film with cash by mail, and intercepting the envelope when it arrived. But she kept two, the one of Otto, slightly bent over and smiling to pick up his shirt and back-lit by the wine shed loft window and the one that Otto had taken of her with her parasol, slipping both into her volume of *Jane Eyre*, a place she knew that Blue would never look.

When a daughter was born, Beatrice and Blue named her Marlise and christened her twice, once in Virginia, in Fincastle, where Blue's parents lived, and then again at the Close, though of course Otto did not attend, he being a squatter of sorts, not part of the family circle the way that Ida and Brut Eble were. The Lutheran minister who had married them presided at the christening. The Wellses could or would not make the trip, perhaps because Beatrice insisted on giving her daughter her own last name, just as she had kept it for herself. "Marlise Schade" is what she had written on the birth certificate there in the hospital, emerging from the twilight sleep of anesthesia to name and, in this one way, claim her daughter as her own, an act of will witnessed by the somewhat disapproving but also surprisingly sympathetic nuns. Cole had also been unable get away from Virginia for the Close christening (he hadn't made it to Fincastle either), and even Maurice, the appointed godfather, was tied up on the West Coast. Lucky, Bea thought, imagining the flare-up that might have ensued between Maurice and Blue if he'd shown up. Though that might have been good cover, she thought, for the truth.

Back at the Close for the christening, Beatrice longed to go to Otto. Blue lurked, continued his vigilance, kept close

to her. She wondered if Otto had heard about her pregnancy, her daughter, the baptism at the Close, and if he suspected the baby might be his, or if he thought it might be Blue's, which would be an entirely other kind of grief. Surely the dates told all. She was stricken with remorse that they'd not once communicated since she'd left the Close in August. No doubt her insisting on this Close christening despite Blue's objections ("Christ, why bother with a christening at all," he'd said. "We don't believe in anything, do we?") had something to do with an instinctive, poorly thought out desire to, to what? Leave Blue? Reclaim the truth of her brief taste of freedom and unleashed desire? Give up all pretense and move in with the strange, quiet, older umbrella maker in a cabin in the woods of her own family's superannuated farm? And what about her baby, her precious Marlise? Would Beatrice be allowed to keep her under such circumstances? Overwhelmed by guilt, flooded with uncertainty and hormones, she did nothing.

She did nothing except love Marlise passionately, reading to her, singing to her in her bassinet, nursing her, sleeping finally only in the baby's room, the little body curled in her arms at night as she grew, cherishing the memory of Otto most in Marlise's shapely ears and hands, her piercing gray eyes. The marriage endured, and who can say what happened exactly that Christmas they had driven up to the Close. Marlise, still a toddler, had stayed behind at the big house in the care of Ida while, on an especially overcast and bitterly cold evening between Christmas and the new year, Bea and Blue drove to a party in Princeton to see old undergraduate friends of Blue's, and after, what—too many cocktails? a fight? a frigid silence mixed with Blue's tendency to

drive recklessly?—there had been the accident. When their car was towed by hook and chain from the sluggish waters of the icy Raritan Canal, the police had said that, surprisingly, there seemed to have been no evidence of panic or struggle—as many believed to be true of their marriage as well.

The Close, March 1971

All day Marlise had watched a bruised sky lower over the fields until the snow began to fall, the house quiet except for the clank of the radiators, the distant grumbling from the cellar furnace far below. As the daylight failed, she felt herself fading also. Utterly unsupervised these past weeks, battered by Silas's letters, she had begun to let go. What had she last put into her mouth? And when?

For days she'd played games with herself to stay awake. She tried to remember everything she could, starting with her childhood and all the way up through Silas. She remembered someone's freckled arms holding her. It was more a smell than anything. The young nun at school who called her Marvelisa. A drawing she'd done of a horse. "Spirited," her teacher had written on the back. "Keep drawing!" How Silas said he saw her in all her ages. Daughter. Mother. Lover. She imagined kissing Silas. How she longed to do that; why had she not? She imagined doing more with Silas. She remembered pulling him, shirtless and bleeding from the ward laundry sink. She ached for him. She worried. Who would protect him now. Was he still fucking Nina? She thought about poor Nina, whom she hardly knew. What it must be like to be out of control like that. But of course she herself was wildly out of control, despite the uneaten soup, the unopened boxes of crackers, the refusals that had once made her feel alive. Books, birds, even the shield of hunger

had withdrawn its power. She was too exhausted to decline the loss.

She looked out the window at the blue snow. Why had she never left this house? Why hadn't she tried to find a phone? Could she reach the ward even if she knew the number? Was Silas even there?

She tried doing her times tables, but got stuck in the 8s. She recited the alphabet backwards. With a pencil from her purse, she wrote "phone is in shed" on the back of Dr. Lance's card in case she forgot what Ida had told her and she could make her way out. After the snow. In case of emergency. She got out her books—the children's books she'd found, the bird guide, her Mother's copy of *Jane Eyre*. She traced her fingers over her mother's signature, set down years ago inside the front cover before she, Marlise, had even been born or thought of.

Out fell the photograph, Beatrice with her umbrella. Marlise fingered its white, scalloped border and stared into her mother's heart face. One corner of the picture felt off, uneven. With her fingernail, she jimmied the edge until she realized it was stuck to another photograph. Two pictures, stuck together, back to front. Carefully, with the fingernail of her thumb, she pried the two apart. How had she not noticed this before? In one hand, she held her beautiful mother. In the other, a man naked from the waist up looked back at her. He was standing in what appeared to be a barn or shed, a loft, back-lit by an open window, bent slightly, as though to pick up something from the floor, smiling over his shoulder out of the kindest eyes she had ever seen.

South Jersey, March 1971

Zeno Mastrogiovanni loved a blizzard. The chaos drew him. In the afternoon, he'd wrapped the wheels of his pick-up with studded tire chains, just in case he felt like taking a drive later. He listened to the forecast on the radio, and ate a TV dinner, Salisbury Steak and a triangle of mashed potatoes stained with something brown. Gravy. Zeno liked the way the foil tray was sectioned off into triangles so that the corn and potatoes didn't touch the meat. He fidgeted a bit and thought about watching something on television. He checked the window, white on white. He decided he would, after all, just go out for a little drive. See who else was out on the road in all this mess.

The pelting snow, flecked with sleet, clarified the storm that had lately been whipping around inside his own head like scalded milk. Panfuls of it, boiling, his mother had flung at him, to quiet him. Half of his face bore the shiny, pulp-red shape of one of those assaults. Or the metal trays of ice cubes she'd cracked over his head when he was a boy, little and thrashing in anger and frustration on the floor.

The snowstorm made a curtain, like those he used to hide behind in the dark houses of his childhood, under coats in the closet, a tablecloth, beneath the bed, behind draperies whenever he felt something agitating against him, or secretly inside him. What that roil was then, he'd be hard-pressed to say. But since he'd come back from Nam, he felt it all the time.

The snow came down clean, cold, obliterating, unlike the jungle, which at first had felt like utter freedom but then had been another kind of perpetual caul, suffocating. He'd enlisted finally, having somehow escaped the draft, and didn't last long. Erratic behavior had been given as the reason for the temporary disability discharge of Zeno and two other men in his unit, and he knew the higher ups had gone easy on them, maybe because everyone was doing things they shouldn't, but especially bad had been that business with those hooch maids who turned out to be little girls. How he'd gotten off for that he didn't know. Yes, that had been especially bad. One girl, in particular, was so small Zeno could hold her off the floor while he made her do things to him and he did things to her. Who could tell how old anyone was over there, with their teeth blackened, their little tits and tight holes in the haze of torpor, Thai stick, Red Tiger beer, and worse.

So here he was, on the verge, barely employable, out on the road, cutting through the white welter in the hot blunt cab of his jacked-up pick-up, huge tires wrapped with metal. The few other vehicles he passed were mere insects crawling, faintly aglow in their own shrouds. Was he heading north? Jersey City? Tess? Maybe so. He hadn't decided yet. The bitch.

At a deserted service station on Route 130 he pulled over to drink, the whiskey making a furnace of his thick ribcage. He was supposed to go light on the booze with these new pills they'd given him to help with his temper, the nightmares.

The storm was worsening, he felt it, and he considered turning back. And then this dumb-shit faggot in an overcoat appeared out of nowhere from an old Jaguar already smothered in snow, fist pounding his window, wondering

if he might get a ride, just a short ways up 130 then a short jog over was where he needed to be, if he was already going that way.

Zeno knew the smell of death. And this guy with the wet gray ponytail spiked with ice burrs gave it off in spades. Sick. Already a goner. He watched as Cole Schade struggled up into the passenger seat, panting, clapping snow off his gloves and removing them, extending a thin, cold white hand, nails fastidiously clipped, introducing himself, announcing his destination, small farm, old family place, nobody there, trying to get there, on the road all afternoon from Virginia, but the car just couldn't make it through the blizzard. "More than they were calling for, ha-ha, right?" said Cole, setting a small suitcase on the floor at his feet, grappling around for a seat belt.

Zeno said nothing, watched the slight alarm that crossed Cole's face as he took in Zeno's blistered visage in the dim light of the dashboard. He took another long swig, thinking okay. Change of plans. Zeno was bored. An opportunist. "Show the way," he said, pulling a couple Black Beauties out of his jacket pocket and swallowing them without drink before shifting into gear. Tranquilizers be damned. He'd squirreled away the speed for just such an adventure. In the rear-view mirror, the old guy's abandoned Jag disappeared behind them in a tickertape of sleet.

The Institute, March 1971

If Marlise had had the energy to read through all of Silas's missives, she would have perhaps had an inkling of his plan to come and find her. By early March, Silas had been off his medication for over a week, only pretending to swallow and then hoarding the damp tablets in a sock in his duffel bag. The high he'd felt, coming out of the drug sludge, was so private and exquisite he felt his wrist scars burning at their closed seams. He'd known for a while that he needed to get to Marlise, had to see her, make sure she was okay, and that the only way he could pull this off would be for him to clear his head. He knew the risks of doing that: first the high, but then the dip, the voices, perhaps even hallucinations, though it had been a while since he'd had any of those. Suicidal thoughts blah blah blah. But the sharper his mind became, the more he realized that Marlise really might in danger. Why else had she not written to him? Not responded to any one of his letters? Of all the things they talked about, her choice of starvation was something he'd weirdly respected. He had needed her, in a way, to be frail, to require him, and in this way to protect him from himself and from the unwanted attention he always seemed to attract. He had been selfish, he saw that now. He fiercely wanted Marlise to live. He would find and save her.

He was also afraid of the electric shocks, which his doctor said his parents had agreed to have done right there at The

Institute, rather than to risk moving Silas again. They might move him later, but first the sequence of shocks over a period of days, then weeks, commencing soon. No mention of bringing him home, whatever home meant, wherever it was. The shock rooms were in the basement of The Institute; you had to pass them on the way to Psycho-Drama in the evenings. Silas missed Marlise sitting beside him with all her inchoate desire, longings that he believed only he could interpret and translate back to her. Plugging into her wordless want short-circuited something dangerous in him, and he needed to find her before his head started filling up again with the noise, directives, static, and paranoid arias that unfailingly landed him in trouble.

It ended up being easy. After breakfast one overcast morning he'd lifted a pack of matches from a nurse's sweater pocket hung on a chair. Near the end of that day's morning OT session, right before lunch, he'd ignited some paint rags soaking in a bucket by the stand of easels. When oily smoke and fumes rose up and people began milling about, some warbling, screaming, the orderlies herding the patients toward the door, he'd slipped out of one of the cracked windows by the overheated macramé station with its hemp veil of plant hangers, (there were advantages to being small), grabbed the duffel bag and pea coat he'd stashed behind a bush in the courtyard the day before, walked right down the semi-circular entrance drive, took a hard right back along the stone and iron fence, and started off, walking first, barely concealing the adrenaline pumping inside, he had to seem normal out there on the street, under the sooty girders of the El, and then finally he was running, elbows high, breath huffing, toward the center city. When the day lengthened he

started hitching rides along the Schuylkill, and by dark he was in Burlington, New Jersey, at a bus shelter beside a diner, where a middle-aged trucker dropped him off, handing him a wool cap from the glove box that he said he didn't need and a twenty dollar bill.

"Get something to eat," he'd said, "and then go home, son. Get a haircut."

The icy snow that had started an hour ago was descending steadily, sticking to the roads. And Silas, soaring with unleashed serotonin and inspired by the wild storm, had decided he was never going back. He would not be locked up again. He would not be shocked into oblivion. He would find his Marlise. He would live and die with her, making art, safe from his family, the draft, the voices, closeted wherever she was, there in her mythic Paradise.

South Jersey, March 1971

"You see," the dying guy was saying to Zeno, "it's like these clocks I've got. They all hang on the same wall, and after I rewind them, their pendulums—pendula, pendulae?—always synchronize for a few days until they wind down. The pendulums swing in opposite directions but in perfect time. That's what's going on with me, I can feel it. It's cellular. Did you know that if you added up the surface area of all your guts they'd be roughly the size of two tennis courts put together? And all of these cells and microbes and things, they regulate each other. Like clockwork. It's what I've always counted on, myself. Regulation. And then knowing when the time is right."

The more the sicko with the ponytail rambled on about bacteria and intestines and homeopathy and fucking *pen-dooolaayy*, all the while tapping to ten on the dashboard, stopping, then tapping another ten times and then again, the more Zeno, clean out of whiskey, buzzing on the speed he'd popped, wanted to shove the old guy out of the cab, leave him right there in a stinking, steaming hole in the snow. The windshield was splotchy; the wipers could barely keep up, the Ford's headlights hung, two spindly ghostlike arms, like a sleepwalker creeping into the whiteness ahead. They were the only two people on the road. Zeno could lean across, open the door, push him out. No one would ever know. Not about *this* crime, anyway. Lighten his load.

Weeks might pass before anyone would find the ponytailed asshole, frozen to death in heaps of ploughed snow beside the highway.

"Put you out of your misery."

"What's that you say?" Cole said, looking up from his collar, as if he'd been asleep.

Good God, he did not look good. Yellow in the face. Zeno had not realized he'd spoken aloud. "Nothing," he said. The goner was just talking to himself, he realized. Not worth the trouble. At least, not yet.

"Shut it, will you? I got to concentrate. How much farther is this place?"

Cole peered out of the window, looking for something familiar. A green sign loomed up. "Oh, here, get off right here. It's, it's just ahead now, five, ten miles maybe. A turn-off. Then be looking for a big tree. On the left. That'll be the Paradise Plane Tree. And the oyster shell road. That's where you'll turn in. House is down by the river."

Right-o, Zeno thought. Paradise plane tree. Oyster shell road. Shit. What century did this guy creep out of?

Two things were keeping Zeno going. One, the old guy talked about a big house, some kind of mansion, and nobody much around. Zeno was nothing if not, as he always liked to brag, an opportunist. An optimist. Might be something fun there for him. At the very least: hooch. He could use another drink. Or something to lift, nick, pawn off later after he ditched this guy. He knew it was getting to be a problem, the stealing, but clepping things was another way he calmed his inner storms. He'd had the one stateside arrest already, when he'd just gotten back from Nam. Just a warning, the cop had known his father. But Zeno was off the grid tonight.

Who could possibly know? Second reason: gas. This farm place had a gas pump, apparently. If Zeno was going to make it much farther tonight, he'd need to refuel. Why not refuel for free?

The Close, March 1971

Since dawn Marlise had not ventured downstairs. As the storm advanced, not even the birds visited her sills, and when she could no longer see past the squall to the river she'd taken two long, hot, consecutive baths. As always, she took care not to rub too hard on the inside of her wrist, where Silas had drawn a small birdcage with a laundry marker the night they'd said goodbye, weeks ago now, back in another world. A blizzard of minutes ago. The scribbles on her arms and thighs had faded, and now Silas's drawing was disappearing, too. Her wrists burned.

Soaking in the scalding water, Marlise could not get warm. She sat afterwards on the toilet, wrapped in a blanket and steam, and tried to pee. As the room cooled she saw on the window opposite what appeared to be letters. She stood to better see. Her small spill of urine in the bowl was the color of wet brick. Like first menstrual blood, though Marlise hadn't had a period for almost a year. On a lower pane of the room's one window, someone had written on the steamed-up glass "HELP ME." But had written it backwards, as if to be read from without. Who had written this? Was it Marlise herself who had done so? When? And for whom? She could not remember. Perhaps she was just imagining things. What day was it? She'd been trying to keep track, since she knew her birthday was coming. Fifteen. On the fifteenth. The Ides. Would anyone remember? Would she?

It was snowing heavily by then, the window white with gusting curtains of flake, the road below already erased. Back in her bed, she piled on top of her bones all of the bedding, towels, and clothing she could find. She had already slipped into unconsciousness when evening fell. She was dreaming of nothing when somewhere, a power line went down, and the bulb she'd left burning beside the cot sparked out, the furnace stories below guttered, and the water hissing in the large ornate radiator across the room went still, then gradually, decidedly, grew cold.

*

The storm had not knocked out power at the marina as it had up at the big house, but after securing the tarps and the beached outboard, feeding the one-winged owl, cloistered and ruffled in her pen of chicken wire, the dead mice from two traps, and checking on the chickens flustered in their loft, and the old turtle, and after bringing in some extra wood, Ida had pulled down and climbed up early into the Murphy bed. She lay a while, smoking her pipe. What about the strange thin girl alone up in the big house? Earlier in the week, the box from the week before was mostly untouched. What would Beatrice think of her sick little girl left alone with just Old Ida to watch over her, and not very well at that? All that time she'd spent with Beatrice in this very kitchen, talking, as though she were her very own daughter. "You'll be all right," Ida said aloud, as though the girl could hear her. Plenty of heat, food for a week or more. Still. Maybe I should have brought you back here, she thought. Might try to get over there in the morning, when the storm lets up. Pull out the old snowshoes I used to wear to walk to school in such weather. If they were still in one piece,

if their cross-hatch threads still held. If I can even get to the shed. Not as young as I used to be. How old am I now, anyhow?

From the room's one window Ida couldn't see a thing. Not the sky. No light from Windy Bill's shack. Not the crick. She wondered about the old umbrella maker. Otto. Years since she'd seen him to talk to him, though she knew he walked out to the road to catch the bus to Riverside now and then. Errands. Groceries. I'd know it, if he had died, she thought. Windy would have known and told me. Otto's ancient uncle was long gone, of course. Ida was too tired, she thought, to be in charge of anything, not any of them, especially not with this smothering tick of snow, coming down harder now, with strong wind. An old-fashioned storm, Biblical, and odd for its being almost spring by the calendar, and the likes of which she hadn't seen in years.

Ida was drifting into a dream of her brother Stanley, alive again, pulling a sledge behind unsaddled Bucky, flattening out a path so she and Beatrice's mother Lena could pass along the creek road to school, Ida with her funny Indian paddle shoes, gift of one of her father's friends, a man from out west who lived now in Philadelphia and came over to gun sometimes in the Close woods in winter. Like tennis or badminton rackets they were, strapped onto her high-buttoned boots, and as the snow piled up above the horse's shoulders on either side of the sledge, steam plumed from Bucky's nostrils, and all three children laughed, giddy in the sun-brilliant dare of a new world suddenly everywhere.

*

Through the woods behind the marina and up beyond the old vineyard, Otto was also having trouble drifting off to

sleep, though in general he enjoyed a snow storm. He had plenty of food laid by. The shovel was in the house. Lights, heat. Woodstove if the electricity failed, and seasoned wood cut and inside too.

I'm dying, he thought. He was not afraid. He'd had a good life. Losses, yes, sacrifices, sure. But also this place to live in, and work to do.

And he'd had his great adventure, the beautiful Beatrice, their summer of transport. How lucky he'd been to have had that time with her, and, after having had the privilege of consoling her as a child, to have had the great good luck to love her so completely as a woman. Not every person alive is allowed that. That kind of pleasure, that privilege, that kind of time.

After Beatrice had gone, it's true that he'd had a difficult spell. Desire and jealousy tortured him. As had a sadness deeper than any he'd ever known. Guilt, too. Had he been wrong to love her so, married as she was to another man? Sorrow that she had drowned. At other times, self-pity got the best of him. One night, after some wine, angry, he'd made a fire in an oil can out back and burned the fairy house, the pavilion, all the silly umbrellas. He watched the grapevine, the twine, the cork, the silks and damask and bamboo meld into a neon crucible. Sparks of that enchantment snapped and flickered high into the darkness, like fireflies or stars. The constellations of freckles on Beatrice's back. He grabbed at a spark and trapped it in his blistering hand. He wouldn't open it again until the light extinguished.

South Jersey, March 1971

Salvadore Rossi, a line cook at the Burlington Diner on Route 130 had come off his shift early and was struggling to get his truck out of a steep drift of snow beside a dumpster when Silas—his newly acquired cap doing what it could against the stripping gusts coming in horizontally now, duffel bag hugged to his chest—picked his way across the parking lot from the bus shelter and asked about a ride.

Unbelievably, the young man, without looking up as he threw fistfuls of cat litter under the back tires, shouted over the gale that, no, he did not know any Marlise Schade, but yeah, he knew the Close, old place, no one living there now that he knew of, but his Poppi had worked there packing peaches in the old days. He was heading down that way, to Cinnaminson. Would give Silas a lift at least part of way in return for a push and help with these blasted tire chains.

Shivering uncontrollably once he was seated in the warm truck, Silas was himself too excited to speak. That he was near, getting ever nearer now, to Marlise, coursed palpably through his body. His palms and feet itched. Was something on fire? He glanced at the dashboard ash tray. Stone cold.

Salvadore the line cook began fiddling with the radio dials, flipping through channels of static. "Nothing," he said. "Fucking storm."

"Line Cook" was probably too fancy a moniker for this gentleman, thought Silas, who hadn't registered the young

man's real name. If he'd even offered it. More like smash burger. Or Tuna Melt.

They were moving slowly, one of just a few vehicles still out on the highway. Way up ahead an elephantine snowplow churned, and they crept along in its wake. At one point Tuna Melt's truck seemed to be standing still, and Silas thought he might jump out of his skin. He swallowed. What was burning? Something in the engine, maybe, as the truck leaned into the wind?

"You mind?" Silas asked, reaching for the radio dial. Tuna grunted. "Go ahead," he said.

When Silas touched the metal radio panel his fingers gave off a loud pop, sizzled, and briefly sparked. The cab filled with the acrid stench of scorched hair. Silas bolted back in his seat. "Jesus," said Tuna. "What the fuck."

Before Silas could reply, the radio burst into sound, and the rich, crackly warp and weft of an Italian opera soared into the cab. Silas saw the sound waves as ornate swirls, magenta, pluming out of the dashboard speakers.

"Oh my God," said Silas. "Do you hear that?"

A baritone was singing in English. *"More happy love! More happy, happy love!"* It was John Keats. The urn poem! The soloist's voice swooped and eddied, silver now, passionato. Silas began to sing along. *"For ever warm and still to be enjoy'd, For ever panting and for ever yooo-oounnggg!"*

The cab was completely silent except for the tick of snow and the swipe of wipers. "Oooo-kay," said Salvadore under his breath. He gave Silas a sideways look.

"Look, guy," he said, tentatively. "I hear nothing."

The truck crept on. How to stay calm, plan his next move. What to do about this shaking hitchhiker, swaying and

singing in the seat beside him? Salvadore started to edge toward the roadside drifts left behind in the wake of the snowplow slowly moving away, up ahead.

I think right about about here, Salvadore thought to himself, downshifting and drifting over to the side of the road, tires grunting in the deep snow. Without looking at Silas, he said aloud, "This where I'm gonna need you to, to uh to vacate my vehicle."

At this point the faint, blinking lights of the snowplow up ahead of them completely disappeared from view. Tuna and Silas were in the middle of nowhere. Not another car or truck in sight.

Silas didn't hear Tuna. His eyes, the lashes glittery with tears, were closed, and he was conducting along to music only he could hear, both arms batting the air.

"What the?" Salvadore took a deep breath and shoved a brief flicker of compassion to the very darkest back of his mind. A hippy, clearly. Obviously on drugs. This storm was crazy enough; he had to get shut of this nut, get himself home safe. Paula would be at home waiting for him, with the baby, worried sick.

"You're not far now," said Salvadore as he continued to inch as close as he could get to the roadside. "The Close, it's just a mile or so down that road up there, that break in the woods. A short ways down that road. Right there. You'll see woods first, then fields, then a long driveway to the house."

"*Who are these coming to the sacrifice?*" Silas was continuing to warble along to the inaudible music as the orchestra swelled. His face was beatific in the dashboard snow-light.

He continued to hum as the pick-up shuddered to a stop, motor still running at the drifted shoulder of what road was

left. Tuna reached across Silas to wrench open the door. The cab filled with a puff of light snow.

Later, remorseful that he hadn't taken the time, gotten off the highway and seen the poor sucker to his destination, after all it was just a short drive to the old farm, Salvadore would like to think that he had not more or less pushed the guy out into the snow. Which he had.

In the weeks afterwards, Salvadore would pause over a grill of flipped burgers or while shaking the fry basket, and hope the crazy punk had gotten where he needed to go, found what he was looking for. For a while, he even checked the local papers. No word of anybody freezing to death in the "Blizzard of '71." A couple of dogs did perish, though. It really was a crying shame, he thought, the way some people treated their animals.

"You take it easy," was what he said now to Silas. Good luck to you, Loony Tunes, he sighed to himself. God bless.

But peering back up into the cab from the snowy road, what Silas saw come out of Tuna's mouth were the words "Thou still unravish'd bride of quietness!" The letters floated in the air of the cab like the lit end of a sparkler tracing words in air on a summer's night.

"Oh, thank you, kind Sir Tuna, Finest of Fish!" said Silas extravagantly, his tears mixing with the heavy snow. "Thank you, thank you, thank you so very much for the kindness of your conveyance."

And then he turned, a small hunched shape in a watch cap, shouldering a duffel, and disappeared into the squall as Salvadore Rossi slowly edged back into the highway's one cleared lane, and crept shamefully away toward Cinnaminson.

The Close, March 1971

In Marlise's dream, there under the pile of garments and blankets in the high, dark, freezing room, time slid back, and it was again just coming up on winter and the solstice, evening cauterizing the sky over Mill Creek & beyond, the hospital's blue smokestacks pouring forth the residue of laundry, baths, meals, heat. Or was it Barton she saw, with its brick arcades and snowball fights, or her childhood playground, the nuns billowing black sails at the margins, huddled together for warmth? And Marlise was walking and walking the shadowed infinity paths of the courtyard waiting to be called inside—to meals, to meeting, to class, to chapel. This was the hour she felt most herself, skeletal downy limbs a hidden insinuation inside one heavy veil or another, the beaver coat, or childhood snowsuit, or head wrapped in wool scarves the OT techs knitted for her, air burnt with dinners being delivered, dinners she would not eat as she tramped along, sometimes running, sometimes carrying her dead mother like a baby in her arms, Beatrice was so wet and cold, so heavy!, the sparkle of little lit Christmas trees on counters of the nursing stations reflected in the tower's windows. White thread of her breath. "*O come O come,*" a robin sang to her from a garden path, clear bright Advent song of longing from the deep past, "*and ransom captive Israel.*" Around and around she took her body, sometimes breaking into a trot, sometimes barely shouldering the cold. In lonely exile here. "*Are you ready,*" Sly sang, and

the crowd clicked its upraised cigarette lighters into communal flame. "*Are you ready?*" A crush of flannel, sweat, urine. "*If you get bit, don't hate the bite.*" And so forth. "*Rejoice, rejoice.*" The world cold and bright and alive with a hunger that had, for so long, been all that she owned. What a waste.

*

At that moment, Otto, too, was still awake in bed. He thought he heard a knocking at the cabin door, but he listened again. Just wind in the snowy trees. The racket in his chest slowed. He remembered the lantern of the hand-trapped spark. It had taken months for his blistered palm to heal. He touched the scar. I'll sleep better if I put the porch light on, he decided. As if anybody would be looking for him, or even cared that he was still alive.

*

"Anybody live around here?" Zeno asked after he'd knocked the snow off the single gas pump shrouded beside one of the sheds, filled the Ford's big tank until the gasoline spilled over in the dark and snow, no way to measure it, onto his glove, the smell sharp and incendiary, and he'd climbed back into the cab. He'd left the motor running while he pumped. His passenger was fading on him, he could see that. The big house was ahead, a dark bulk, a few dozen yards off along the barely perceptible brush and river. Some very faint lights blinked a way, way off across the water, but this place was frozen shut and dark for miles. Not a lit window anywhere.

Cole shook himself, looked out the window. "Oh, yes, why, we're here. No, nobody's around these days. Some old people living off in the woods. Out along the river. Usually there's

a pole lamp that comes on at night by the house. Line must be down."

"No need for you to stay," Cole had said to Zeno after Zeno had inched the truck up beside the house. "Thank you for the lift. Life-saver. Much obliged."

Much obliged, buttwipe? Part of Zeno, fraying as the buzz turned thin, edgy, very much did want to be off. Get on his way. But this prissy gentleman annoyed him. Ticked him off bad. So no, he'd stick around a bit. He wouldn't leave, not just yet.

"I'll just make sure you get inside safe, the power out and all," Zeno said, thinking how fake he sounded, what an asshole he was. What did the sick guy want anyway? That interested him. Why were they here?

It was taking Cole way too long to gather up his bag, lurch his way out of the truck into the thick fall of snow and up onto a side porch through the wind and drifts. "The key is always kept here," he was saying, swiping in the dark at a snow-capped metal milk box beside the door. Zeno, standing behind him, grew more and more impatient as Cole fumbled around. Why not just turn around right now, Zeno thought. Get the fuck on the road, leave the loser, head back out into the storm, up the highway, clear his head. Find Tess. See what she had to say for herself. He reached into his pocket, palmed and swallowed a couple more pills. He had two Black Beauties left. Needed to pace himself.

"Oh shit, for God's sake." The old goat had slipped and fallen, making a surprising thud for someone with not many bones inside his overcoat. Furious, Zeno wrested the metal milk box from Cole, heaved its sharp corner at a glass panel beside the door, reached in, wrenched the deadbolt, and

shouldered himself inside, kicking and rolling Cole along the floor in front of him as he went.

Inside was almost as cold as outside, and quiet as a grave. The windows white. While Cole whimpered and struggled on the floor, Zeno went out to his truck for his flashlight. The keys were still ticking in the ignition; he turned off the motor but decided to leave the keys there. Might need to be leaving soon. He could still smell the gasoline on his coatsleeve, strong through the falling snow.

Zeno stepped over Cole and began to look around the house, the flashlight sketching over sheeted sideboards, chairs, and bookcases. He peered under the linens. He opened drawers, cabinets. Empty. No silverware. No booze. Nothing light, nothing liftable. Nothing here he could tote off easy.

Abandoned place. Pathetic. But in the kitchen, he found Ida's box of food. Corn Flakes. Cans of soup. Macaroni. Crumbs on the counter. A greasy bowl in the sink. In the fridge, a carton of milk. Zeno sniffed it. Fresh. Someone had been here recently. Someone was maybe expecting this cocksucker, moaning on the floor.

Zeno checked a light switch. Nothing. He could see his own breath. He could feel the uppers kicking in.

Behind him, Cole had propped himself up against a wall. The door was still open, light sparkly bits blowing inside, onto the floor, the broken glass shards of the window. Zeno should just go. He would. Yet why not take a quick pass through the upstairs rooms. Could be something there—piece of jewelry left behind? Some small change in a drawer? There was the ring he'd stolen from an elderly lady a month ago. It had been easy to slip it from a two-tiered, open velvet case and into his pocket while he was fixing her master bedroom sink

as a sideman on a plumbing job. And Tess had appeared so happy with it when he'd presented it to her, along with a proposal. She'd hold onto it, she said, the ring, admiring its glinty stones. She'd think about it, such a big decision, but she'd let him know soon. It had been weeks now, and no word from the cunt. Zilch. Zip. She wouldn't return the calls he'd left for her, at home, at the restaurant. Stop calling here, Mr. Zeno, her dick boss Ravi at The Pointe Bar & Grill had said to him that very morning when he'd last tried. For all he knew, she'd pawned the ring by now. Skipped town, gotten a new job. New sucker boyfriend to screw over. Why was he with her anyway? Too old, face already lining up, female bits all saggy. Zeno started upstairs.

*

Things were happening inside Silas's body. Having waded through the high drifted margins of Route 130, he stumbled for about twenty minutes down a side road knee deep in snow. The cold was helping to calm his mania, and when he saw the stand of woods Tuna had said to look for, he plunged into them. The canopy of branches kept the snow-fall lighter there, and he moved more quickly in what he hoped was the direction of Paradise Close. Just when he felt like lying down in the warm, beckoning quilt of snow to rest, he'd spotted a light blinking through the fret of snow and branches. Marlise. Paradise. Silas bent his head and plummeted toward it.

*

Well, well, well, thought Zeno, what have we here? He looked down at the thin shape of a little girl in a bed in the corner of a third-story room, buried under a pile of blankets. Flashes of

shack light. Bamboo, thick, humid. Hips small and cleft as a gourd. A noise when he'd lifted her. Now here was something very interesting after all. Something light he could carry off. No problem.

He leaned in, sniffed. Soap. Urine. Fever. His crotch stirred.

As Zeno stood with his flashlight in the blacked-out, freezing upstairs bedroom of Paradise Close, weighing his options, the skeletal body of Marlise Schade lay curled on the bed below beneath a pile of blankets, coats, and bath towels. As her potassium levels plummeted, her blood pressure stuttered, and her heart strained to save her. The kidneys she'd gotten functioning again for a while began to blink on and off. Snow crept up the windowsills. The temperature in the room dropped another degree.

Zeno scooped Marlise up, blankets and all. He was hurrying now, down the dark stairs, two flights. Things were coming into focus for him, finally. His eyes shone. In a split decision, Zeno decided to leave by another door in case the sick guy was still conscious by the kitchen exit. He was back. Zeno was back in the game.

*

What was Otto dreaming of when he awoke to a loud pounding and shouting at his door, his head and heart somersaulting, and made his way through the dark toward the lit porch, wrenching open the door without thinking, against any caution or judgment?

Was the snow-capped figure he found, wind-whipped, stamping, shaking, and sobbing on his porch step, Otto himself, come back after all these years as the lost young man he had once been?

As Silas stood, dripping, shuddering in the warm workroom, Otto wrapped him in a wool blanket. Neurochemicals as powerful as the blizzard raging outside flooded the frontal lobes of Silas's brain as the dopamine system of his septal zones went haywire. Synapses that should be working were not. Stuttered speech. Word salad. Otto could not decipher any of it. All he could do was enfold the boy in his arms.

Otto held Silas close, but his mind churned. What to do with this stranger, this man-boy, who shook like a leaf in his arms, a sodden wool cap, stringy wet hair stropping his cheeks, eyes going bright then dull. Their hearts hammered, each to each though clothes and blankets. What to do with this visitor blown in by the blizzard but hold him until his breath slowed, then lead him to the one small bed, remove his coat and boots, cover him with more blankets, touch his shoulder, sit on a chair beside him, keep watch.

Finally, Silas stopped shivering and babbling, and fell asleep. Otto too, at last dozed in a chair beside him, upright in the blue smock he always wore inside the cabin, even for sleep, in case the boy woke and needed something. What had the boy tried to say between bouts of weeping? Cages, shocks, Grecian urns, torsos, beauty, truth, a jumble of names, a sockful of drugs. Otto thought about opening the boy's drenched knapsack, but decided against it. That would not be right.

*

With his light parcel, Zeno made his way as swiftly as he could in the dark, his flashlight turned off now, across the spacious front hall lit with eerie blizzard glow and out and down the steps, the drifts lofty and up past his knees. The

girl in his arms was weightless, hardly breathing. He would just tuck her, quilt and all, on the cab floor until he got good and clear of this god-forsaken place. You are going to be very gentle, Zeno, he said to himself in the voice of his mother. You know you can be, if you just try.

Cole was in the driver's seat of the truck cab, the muzzle of a handgun jammed into his own mouth.

Zeno's instinct was to grip the girl and run. "Oh, no. No you don't, no you don't," said Cole, suddenly wide awake, everything flooding back to him, things he'd forgotten in the press of his own plans: word from Maurice about a month back that Maurice's ward, Cole's sick niece, would be staying alone at the house for a bit under the oversight of Ida. And it struck Cole: the creepiness and danger of this man now dropping a girl wrapped in blankets onto the cab floor. Cole pointed the pistol at Zeno.

Zeno backed away, hands up, unnerved but steady. Only his voice betrayed him, girlish in the thick icy swirl around them, ticky and sharp as needles. "Why don't you go ahead and off yourself." Zeno forced himself to speak louder, deeper. He spit his words out into the wind. "That's why you're here, isn't it? Do it at the old family place before whatever's got you kills you first? Do it. But first get the fuck out of my truck."

"Here's how it's going to go," Cole said, nimbly leaping over the gear shift and the bundle of Marlise on the cab floor and out the passenger door, cocking the gun at the ice-stung, startled face of Zeno, whose limbs had suddenly gone numb. "You are going to get in the truck. You are going to drive us as fast and as safely as you can to the hospital across the river. I will tell you exactly where and when to turn. If you so much as swerve or take off in the wrong direction, if you try

anything at all, I will shoot you, first in your pathetic cock and balls, and then between your eyes."

Away from the house with its old, enclosed tree they went, then, back past the gas pump, the sheds, churning through drifts up the oyster shell drive, the storm still rocking the Ford, the wipers laboring, the cab heater blasting, Marlise motionless, wrapped in blankets at Cole's feet, his gun pressed to Zeno's crotch.

As they neared the end of the long lane, just as they were about to leave Paradise Close and turn out onto the River Road and barrel toward Delanco and the drawbridge that would take them into Riverside, to the emergency room of the very hospital where Bea and Cole had been born so many years ago—just as the Paradise Plane tree loomed up out of the ghostly gusts—something whooshed toward the windshield, thumping it hard, hovering, holding itself a long second right there in front of them, making a blue crux in the white welter, its off-kilter wingspan wide as an angel's.

"Shit," Cole said. "Owl."

Silence for a moment in the truck. Then Cole pushed the gun into Zeno's temple.

"Next left," he said.

Zeno, jaw clenched, gripped the wheel and drove.

PART TWO

Shenandoah Valley

The Print Shop, 2000

Trey "Tee" Handel had come to her in need. An assistant professor at a Virginia university, he had a new book of poems forthcoming, and it required cover art; a colleague had recommended Emma Miles, a 40-something professor in the Studio Art Department, and a series of prints she'd done, birds trapped in houses, churches, subway stations, currently on view at the University's art museum. An exchange of office-to-studio phone calls and emails brought him, near the end of spring term, to the open door of the print shop, a long, tall-ceilinged addition at the back of a Gothic hall of painting studios.

Often he returned to this moment, wanting to remember it exactly. Not to embellish. To be faithful. The full-frontal, overwhelming acrid atmosphere of acids, solvents, resins. The dank musk of ink. Rackety ventilation fans. Someone playing De La Soul on a CD player. Light from tall windows falling like fables across tables, sinks, three hulking presses, a tall shelf of limestone slabs. Cases of type. Art books in teetering stacks. A hooded bath of acid.

Four or five students were working, one pinning dripping paper to a clothesline, another adjusting, then readjusting a plate, then covering it with a blanket of felt on the bed of a press. Several heads bent over rectangles of zinc and copper, beveling edges of plates with rasps, drawing with needle-tipped pencils Tee would learn to call styluses. Little

baby-nail piles of metal filings on the tabletops. It was a hot May afternoon outside, and in here the fumes immediately had him feeling a little dizzy, off-point. A print shop's like a medieval chemistry lab, she would later tell him, except without the safety features.

She was turned away from him, at a far sink, washing ink off a plate. What he saw first: her small shapely shoulder blades, bare beneath the apron's necktie, the low collar of her blue tank top. Hair—brown?—though later he would know it to be coppery when not drenched with shadow and sweat—piled up in a nest of pins and plastic child's barrettes. A few silver threads mixed in too. Two stray hooks of hair flat against her slender neck. Freckled shoulders. Above the sink, a red box with an exhaust switch, painted with a white skull and cross bones.

He would grow to love approaching her from behind, and it moved him that she liked this, too, unlike other women he'd been with who'd rejected such a gesture as shameful or submissive. Instead, after they became lovers, she would present her strong back to him, its tawny cream and oatmeal shower of freckles, with an authority that brought him to his knees. When he hadn't shaved, she leaned back hard into the stiff brush of his jaw, mouth, as the old record player in his apartment scratched through Maria Callas or Joni Mitchell, or the boom box in his office emitted a soundtrack of Liszt, Ravel, Stevie Wonder. Coltrane.

When Emma Miles turned around that first day in the print shop, wiping her hands with a rag, what did she see? In the dim studio with its high, grimy windows—and given Tee Handel's almost shockingly red hair and the way in his thick black glasses frames the rectangular panes shone white

and obliterated his eyes—he seemed to be transubstantial, on fire, lit like one of Blake's angels or some sort of beseeching, bespectacled saint.

They sat side by side in her cramped windowless office, more of a closet just off the studio, surrounded by piles of art books on tables and floor, the bristling walls stabbed with pins holding up printed pieces of paper, clippings from medical books, field guides, a calendar that was two years old, a postcard of an ocean view over which someone had drawn the criss-cross muntins of a window with black marker and scrawled the words "I don't need a man. Just give me a window over the sink." A bit dizzy from the fumes and his proximity to Emma Miles (he noted that she seemed not to shave under her arms), Tee stammered out his predicament: the need for cover art for a book of his poems. His first book. He praised the prints of hers that he'd checked out at the University gallery. And then, somewhat ceremoniously, shyly, he pulled a thick sheaf of paper from his messenger bag and rested it on top of an empty ashtray on the desk before them.

Beneath the small desk, their knees almost touched. As Tee talked, Em could not keep her eyes off the reddish-white hairs of his forearms, all brushed in the same direction, each a gilt and startled stroke that she felt an irresistible urge to draw, to etch onto a plate, and turn, in the acid's bite, to flame. A desire to wet each glinting follicle with her tongue.

She shook her shoulders. What was happening to her, Emma Miles, middle-aged wife and mother? Her breasts tingled inside her apron in a way that had not since she was a girl and they were first starting to grow. Was this early onset menopause? She'd read somewhere that a kind of

second-wave of, well, horniness could come on as eggs got old. Or perhaps he reminded her of someone? But who?

Emma instinctively hunted for a cigarette in the top desk drawer, then remembered that she had long ago quit smoking. She folded her arms across her chest. "So what kind of stuff do you write?" she asked, to settle herself. "What makes you think your poems would be a good fit with my work?" Tee was usually not one to miss an opportunity to talk about himself or his poems, if asked, as he rarely was, but first was about to disingenuously demur when she added, "and please don't give me that crap about how writers aren't the best people to ask to describe their own work." She nodded her head toward the print shop. "Every one of those undergraduates has to defend their work on a weekly basis. They have to know how to talk about it."

"Maybe," Tee said, suddenly intimidated by this small woman and pressing his knees together to calm them, "we could just read one or two of the poems?" Not trusting his voice, which seemed in danger of vaulting an octave, he said, "maybe *you* could read one? Aloud?" Emma sighed. But she picked up the stack of paper and glanced at the title page.

"The Horologist's Book of Hours? *Horologist? Book of Hours?* Sorry. Don't like it. Smells like, like the academy." Tee winced, he hoped imperceptibly. He slid his fine, strong hands, palm to palm, between his locked knees. He hoped the shaking didn't show. Emma opened to a random page, with, she had to admit, some excitement. She was currently taking graduate courses in English, with an eye toward a PhD, and was just that morning reading the early poems of John Donne. Clearing her throat, she read aloud a poem called "Cocktail Hour." "Hmmmm," she said. She then read, to herself, over

the course of ten silent minutes, "Therapy Hour," "Coffee Hour," and "Power Hour." She liked the poems; they were terse, muscular. No fat in them, a mix of diction, a visual acuity she admired. They shimmered, a bit like this handsome, clearly vulnerable, talented man sitting beside her. She could see from the gentle wrinkles around his mouth and behind those glasses, and a bit of silver at his carroty temples, that he was about her age. Was he married? She saw no ring. Of course she didn't wear one either, printing materials not friendly to metals. Was it just her imagination, or did he seem lonely? And why was she thinking about any of this at all? The poems, the poems, she turned back to them: there was a powerful sense of self-protection in their imagery and their questions that belied a strong reaching for something.

Tee waited, breathless. Em felt his pain. Her own heart hammered. How strange to be feeling things, anything, especially after the past year, when an unusual case of the blues had been nibbling at her, packing her torso with wet leaves. Was it aging? Lack of new direction in her work? Her lovely but increasingly testy and button-pushing teenage daughter? Her self-absorbed, distant husband, a big needy adolescent himself who she knew was having affairs, at least emotional ones? Hormones? She prized what independence she had, and dodged the lurking depression by throwing her energy into her students, her work. And now here she was, flighty and stirred up as a schoolgirl, sitting in a cramped room with a poet whose physical presence and tensile words made her feel she might ignite.

Emma put her ink-stained hands on top of the manuscript to steady them and indicated with her eyes and a quick jerk of her head a scrap of paper pinned right at eye level above

her desk, on which was typed: "There is in us a world of Love to somewhat, though we know not what in the world that should be.... Do you not feel yourself drawn by the expectation and desire of some Great Thing?—Thomas Traherne: <u>Centuries of Meditations</u>."

Tee had by this moment already fallen in love with Em. But before he could ask, "you read Traherne?" She said, "How about *Our Hour*. For the title."

"Done," he said. And then he laughed, surprised at his own immediate yes. When was the last time he'd laughed aloud? But he couldn't stop himself. He took off his glasses and wiped his eyes. Was he weeping? Emma smiled. He looked about twelve years old. That flaming head of hair, the clouded-up eyeglasses. Then she laughed. She was afraid she might cry also, but she did not. They stood. They shook hands.

And this was how it began, if it were possible to narrate such a sourceless and inevitable story. She could have just emailed him some images to look over, of course, on his own, or asked him to pick one of the prints he'd already seen from the Museum show, but instead she offered to bring in work from home and have him come by her office to look through those prints and also some new work. There was a lot of talking at first as they invented ways to protract their time together, deciding upon one print, then choosing another. And he did love to hear her ask about him, to talk about his poems, he was so unaccustomed to that, and she was very insightful about them, in coffee shops, or on long walks that would take them away from campus and into the surrounding neighborhoods, where they peered into people's yards to see what was growing, and never ran out of things to discuss. Then one night after graduation, at the start of

a long weekend between the spring and summer terms, on the cusp of a trip she must take away to visit her husband's family, they met on the mostly empty campus. She unlocked the print shop and led him into the cavernous, empty, unlit space. She locked the door and slipped the deadbolt. She stripped off her jacket, shirt, jeans, everything. She held his hand and led him to a table where she pushed her lithe body against his shirt, his canvas pants, her bare feet tiptoe on top of his boots. "Paint me," she whispered, handing him an opened can of something and a brush. By the time pale warm dawn striped the window they were both naked and red as hennaed brides. They stood close, giggling, kissing, shivering in the lukewarm stream of the studio's emergency shower, exposed to the stilled machinery of the shop, the file of high weakly lit windows, the green treetops, scouring themselves with the orange-scented granular soap used by the printmakers to wash lead and ink and gesso off their hands, as water scarlet as blood streamed in rivulets down their limbs, into the drain.

Tee had no idea what happened at home, with her husband and daughter. She never brought it up; he was afraid to ask. It horrified him to imagine anyone else touching her, so he avoided thinking about it. But the way she drew Tee's fingers, tongue, everything into her every opening, eyes wet with wild discovery, made him believe that what happened between them was as unprecedented for her as it was for him.

She bit him, too, sometimes, her hunger so fierce, though he hesitated to bite back. Why? His reticence, fear, whatever it was, only made her more daring. Sometimes, in their aphagic heights when he could hardy see, she'd strike or slap him. But he was never able to do that in return, even in the

moments when he'd go nearly blind, even when he sensed that she wished that he would give her that, almost more than anything else he could offer.

Wondering how Em managed to hide from her husband her body's evidence, *frottage* was what she called the way her delicate, pinkish patch of pubic hair would form into minute, linted dreds after hours of lying, sitting, standing with him, or scratches, constellations of contusions from chair edge or table top or floorboard, nourished Tee's vague hope that the couple did not have sex, or at least did it in the dark. How little Tee knew about his rival, only that he worked as in a government office in a city two hours away and kept a small apartment there during the week, that his parents lived in Ohio (hers, like Tee's, were deceased), that the husband's name was, of all things, Paul, plain old Paul, Paolo, Pablo, and that Paul was older, or looked older, than the artist who was now Tee's infatuation and obsession. Privately, Tee called Paul "Gray Top" from the one glimpse he'd had of him across campus, fetching Em in a jeep, tall, lantern-jawed and military, with a thick silver crop of buzzed hair, flat on top.

Tee came to treasure any residual pains, nips, bruises she left behind; they became for him fetishes, talismans for the hours he and Em could not be together, and he was sorry when a bruise he'd watch bloom from plum to green to yellow eventually faded away altogether. And the times apart from Emma, sometimes quite long times—weeks, nearly two months that first summer when she traveled to Italy with her family—were surprisingly hard for Tee, who, past 40 himself, had never been married, lived alone, and was by temperament solitary.

He was startled by his sudden loneliness, by the intensity of his jealousy, during these stretches. Known for years by his friends as "the monk" for his habit of turning down invitations to dine out or watch films in favor of staying in to read, listen to music, or edit student work or his own poems, he'd passed through undergraduate and graduate school without lasting romantic entanglement, though since adolescence he'd had several passionate crushes, mostly on unattainable women—his professors, his ophthalmologist leaning in close in the darkened room, pressing the cool mask of the phoroptor to his face, flicking eligible lenses into place as he squinted at a white box of letters on the far wall, the doctor asking is it clearer now, or now? better here—or here? This way? Or this?—and Tee never being able say which, as his lap secretly hardened. For a while he had dated a woman in his department, a scholar on the critical side of things, an avowed feminist who dressed parodically in leopard-skin leggings and shaggy faux fur jackets, and whose scarlet bra straps always seemed to show at Steering Committee meetings, and perhaps not unexpectedly dropped by his office one morning to say that she was moving to Berkeley to live with Heather, one of her former graduate students. Another reason you took the veil, his friends would joke with him afterwards.

Em's hunger for Tee moved him, awakening in him not a need so much, or yen for a solution, like that which had first brought him to her office toting his manuscript of poems in search of cover art, but a dawning awareness of lack, a profound want—something primal, unanswerable, beyond the fact of his being with her. Leaning into the fragrant arc of her back had made him feel that he, orphaned at fourteen, might

belong at last to a story. As for her story, she about whom he was always thinking and about whom the more he knew, the less he knew: Tee had come to realize that Emma Miles, like one of her printed gilt birds beating against the black-etched bars of a claustral house seeking egress, deeply needed to be marked. Marked as in seen. And then she had disappeared, overnight, it seemed—inaccessible to him because, as one of the poets he loved had once written, he had, as lover, and not husband or father, "no rights in this matter."

The Swifts, 2016

They dropped out of a sledge of low cloud, hundreds of sooted angels sculling the dusk. Tee paused to admire them. He was in the midst of a walk along the lower ridge of Orphan Mountain, less a mountain and more a swell in the land that was really called Elliot's Ridge, but Tee had always liked to rename things. Make them his own. An erstwhile poet's penchant, he supposed.

Usually his evening route led below, along the bed of the beck, a stream, or really a braid of small streams, that he'd christened Dredlock Springs, its marshes matted with Indian grass and perfumed with sulfur, a tea-black stream dredged this time of year with fallen leaves, an easy traipse along deer trails, through hedges of wild azalea, mountain laurel, and bayberry, a path which, before he turned back at the Springs, afforded him, especially in late fall and winter, a far-off glimpse of the interstate highway, its quixotic pinpricks of pear-cool headlamps oddly consoling in the dark.

The ridge walk was hard to make with a distracted mind, the paths irregular and criss-crossed with thorny bramble scourges, fallen trees. This late afternoon, too, he was forced to trudge through a fresh fall of wet leaves, knee-high in some places, that had come down in a recent, freakish spate of late-October thunderstorms. He called this part of Orphan Mountain the Long Ago because he often lost his way here, despite his pocket compass and his landmarks—an

old cemetery overgrown with periwinkle and marked off by a circle of stones, an abandoned skull of a house shackled by vines, one wall completely stripped away, exposing an inside grid of rooms, like a ravaged doll's house. The ruin of an old iron furnace. Rutted, precipitous lumber and park service roads gashed with blood-red clay, occasionally traversed by trucks and reckless hot-rodding teenagers, though the only evidence Tee had of the latter were the a few weathered crosses marking a spot where someone had long ago wrecked and died. And an aluminum deer stand, about 50 feet off the path, whose ladder he sometimes climbed so he could perch in a seat, rickety as the carriage of a Ferris wheel, and look out upon a purfled infinity of woods and sky.

He knew that others, hunters mostly, hikers, passed through there, but he never saw anyone. Once he found a bloated *Playboy*, its pages stuck together, wedged into the slats of the deer stand aerie. Another time, a green, corked bottle of urine sitting upright in a rut. Why piss in a bottle, he'd wondered, out there with all the woods around you? And one March morning, long ago, when he'd been sixteen, on one of the rare visits he'd made to this place after his own parents' death but before he'd come back as an adult, he'd encountered the faded turquoise remnants of a parachute and a partly unhinged, rope-wrapped human skeleton wedged high in the mistletoe-infested arms of an ancient oak just coming into leaf. Probably a drug-runner, though it would be years before he thought of that, plastic sacks of something coagulated still strapped to the clavicles. What he thought of then, instead, were the bodies of his own parents, charred beyond recognition amidst the wreckage of his father's prop plane, gone down for no finally

discoverable reason into a ridge of the Alleghenies just two years before.

What he saw, now, if anything, were deer, their flanks darker with winter coming on, and flocks of wild turkey, quail, little periscopes skittering in shoals across his way. If lucky, he'd spot the albino fawn, which on three occasions had stared back at him with red-rimmed eyes from different shaded glades. Yesterday, the knuckled vertebrae of a skinless snake, making a loop of itself.

If he concentrated in the Long Ago, was not too preoccupied with his memories of Em, still fresh lo these many years, the chagrin and loss of her a memory that he worried and polished like a key, or with his work on the clocks in his kitchen workshop, he could find the fork that broke through to the lookout. From there he could see, by late October, if he squinted, the six chimneys of the old house, his house, inherited fifteen years ago from a great uncle, and which, despite its immensity, was partially hidden even in winter by swells and thick mesh of treetops, enisled by its own vast acreage amidst miles of state and national forests in an area known for lightning strikes, chalky screes of iron ore, and hot springs.

And sometimes, like this evening, he would arrive at just the right point on just the right hour in late October to see them again: the swifts on their migration southward. Where did they come from? Where did they go? Honduras? Peru? For a few nights each autumn, the swifts returned to lodge in one of the massive chimneys, the tallest one, closest to the central roof spine at the juncture of the main house and the west wing.

When Tee was inside the house—he inhabited just a small part of it—he lost track of its scale, but seen from above, even

obscured by trees and distance, it was impressive. Seven-bays, two-and-a-half-stories, built on a raised basement, it branched off onto four dramatically different elevations, some opening into broad courtyards that had no doubt once been quite fancy, the many windows of the north façade staring down at a wide lawn with a semi-circular drive, all wildly overgrown, and a balustrated piazza reached by broad curving stairs, crumbling and matted with mosses. There was a conservatory, or sun porch, glinting in last light at one end of the upper story. The whole mansion was covered by a standing-seam sheet metal roof with a copper wash, pierced by shed-roofed dormers on the north elevation and pedimented ones on the remaining sides. There were the six large chimneys, and it was into one of these that the swifts now streamed. The house had been known for over a century as Handel Hall, and there was a carved pillar at the end of the long drive that said as much. When he'd been a disgruntled teenager, sent off to school, Tee used to call the place Handel Hell. Now he called it The Hole.

Generations of migrating swifts had been stopping at The Hole. The morning after the first time he'd witnessed from the lookout their gallows-hour swarming, their majestic, gilt scissoring of the air, their ribbony plummets in twos and threes into the chimney top—after several hundred, he'd stopped counting, so delirious was he with an unaccountable premonition of their significance—a visitation!—he had made his way through the dim, cobwebbed catacombs of the massive fieldstone cellar—even now there were parts of the house he'd not explored—pried loose with a coal shovel the rust and lime-stuck damper, and poked a flashlight into its dark mouth.

Gray, feathered cakes of split quills, bird lime, and insect hulls dislodged and broke apart on the hearthstone at his feet, and though the chimney, long unused, was stories high, and his lamp sketched but a short way up, he could tell that the swifts were not there. Had he dreamed them? Tee knelt in the fragments of pinion dross and feared he might weep.

And yet that very night, as the sun sank into the thinning trees to the west, he was compelled to the ridge to watch for them again, and they magically returned, materializing out of thin air and funneling in black rivers into the flue. They followed this pattern for two more nights, like clockwork, feeding by day, roosting at night, and then on the morning of the fifth day, his ear pressed to the whitewashed cellar mantle at the very heart of that monstrous house, Tee felt them depart a last time with a roar so thunderous he ran the long, dank length of the cellar and emerged panting into the frost and dawn of the south lawn to watch them vanish with the fleet undeniability of a wish, a memory, an eon.

Em, Emma, the M-Bomb had left him that way. One day she had been his, he'd possessed her by all the names he had given to her, owned her love, or felt that he had; then she'd evaporated, was gone forever into an ether of obligations, secrets, a departure whose causes, and his own culpability in creating them, he could, or would, not fathom, own, nor ever truly forgive. Em for "married," he'd think in moments of particular self-pity.

Tee had to admit that his excitement about the way the swifts left but then returned was in some way connected to a wish that Emma Miles would materialize again, repentant and still passionately in love with him. Since that first visitation of the swifts, Tee had read about them, learned that

unlike many birds they can not perch, and instead hang, like bats, and so must all day fly, fly, beating the air, searching, hunting, fueling, never resting, never once stopping until some instinct harnesses them, calls them at sunset in one ecstatic herd, to whatever place—an empty tree trunk, an old, uncapped chimney—the latter more and more rare these days—to roost and flock and shelter and rest. He had watched for them every year after that and seldom missed their return or departure. Once, creeping along the un-electrified tunnels of the west wing cellar with his flashlight, very quietly, so as not to disturb them, he'd shifted aside the plywood plank he'd put up to block light and egress, and for as far up as his beam could reach he saw the swifts hanging there, folded, fat penknives, side-by-side in sleep, their feathers sleek in the fragile cone of his torch beam, cobbling the guano, creosote, and smoke-haunted blackness that tunneled beyond his reach toward the star-clabbered sky.

If Tee had not been so absorbed in thinking on this particular evening about the eighteenth-century English wooden long-case clock opened up and dismantled on sawhorses in his kitchen shop, of the day's puzzlement over the crown wheel and verge, he might have been more conscious of his walk's direction, the reasons for choosing to clamber up the ridge to the lookout. No matter. Here he was again, after all, his breath condensing in the air, arms wrapped around his torso, compelled by tides beyond himself. And if he had not been, there on the chilly, burnished precipice, so caught up in the spectacle of his swifts' annual return, he might have seen, from the chimney at the furthest gable of the far east wing, near the glass conservatory, a pencil trace of smoke rising, then dissolving into the blue brow of the declining year.

The Hole

Tee's earliest memory was of this house. He was visiting his great-aunt and uncle. He was a young boy and should have been asleep, but instead he was in the dark main hall, walking the gauntlet of tall clocks collected by his great-uncle, hulking wooden cases, ebony, mahogany, carved, also brass, some with mirrored and beveled doors, some with clear glass panels through which swags, nooses, necklaces of chains dangled, pendulums shaped like pine cones, plumb hearts, coins rocking back and forth. Each hooded timepiece with its own numeral-scarred moon-face staring across the hallway into immense windows that cast urns of milky moonlight across the floor.

A welter of ticks and whirs, of cogs, teeth, catching imperceptibly, like breath, in their wheels. Hush of dust, of minutes, of a carpet plush with patterned wisteria and antelope.

Tee's boy-shadow crossed them. He tiptoed a long time before stopping at a case slanted like a drafting table, draped and funereal, like a piece of furniture stored for a season. A vitrine. He raised the heavy leather cloth. A light clicked on inside the case when Tee lifted the glass pane of its lid. Inside, a trove of pocket-watches: jeweled, enameled, some pinned open, all seemingly whispering from within, like scallop shells or a fallen star.

He touched the pocket watch with a white rose painted on its onyx lid. So beautiful. But look! Just as he thumbed

the catch, he felt Uncle's raw laughter rise up inside him, the flicked locket opening deftly to show, wreathed by a circle of Roman numerals, a painted priest in collar and black robe, red cock plunged in a skirt-hoisted maiden. And there was at the same time a sudden, pointed silence followed by a deafening, clamorous roar: the tolling hour loosed from countless bells and chimes and cuckoos. Tee dropped the case lid and ran back upstairs to his bed, chased by the choir of the booming midnight hour.

This memory came from a time when the clocks in the main hall and the shelf clocks in the library and sitting rooms, and the painted mantle clocks in his great-uncle's study still worked, were kept going by an itinerant Belgian who came through annually with his felted bolster of needle-like tools. This was before his great-uncle, whose father had been a magnate in guns and sewing machines, had died some years after his parents went up in flames together in the small private plane crash, like in a movie or a novel, and Great Uncle William's wife, who eventually lost her mind, lived there without him, wandering the massive rooms and grounds in her white court shoes and fox-hunting jacket or pressed, pastel shirt-dresses. In those years, while Tee was away under the care of remote trustees in a series of boarding schools and universities, educating himself among other things in the mysterious ways of verse, and then making his way as a new teacher and as a shy, anxious, mostly unrequited lover, his great-aunt's beloved salukis took to stalking the by then torn-up allée of boxwoods and the feces-riddled oriental rugs of the porches, the house, with freshly slaughtered deer legs.

Eventually, the salukis raided the barns, hefting the old woman's horses' limbs and anvils of ribcages about the

property in their slathered jaws. This was before raccoons overtook one wing of the main house; before a spin-off band of the Rainbow people drove an old school bus through the overgrown privet and box mazes, parked by the fountain of Anteros, modeled after the famous "Eros" statue in Piccadilly Circus, and grew an acre of marijuana beyond the clay tennis courts and lower lawn.

Over the better part of two decades, a string of other shiftless and misbegotten, mostly harmless tenants had colonized every nook and cranny of that sprawling mansion under Tee's doddering great-aunt's fragile and much-abused oversight. Finally, after a bipolar denizen of the crumbling carriage house put rat poison in the jug wine of the woman renting space in an adjacent remodeled tool shed, necessitating an emergency stomach-pumping at a regional hospital and a summoning of the police, executors from New York arrived, clearing the house of its mired tenants, hiring a team of locals to sweep out the dung and exterminate the vermin, boarding up whole wings of unused rooms, and removing Tee's great-aunt north to a hospital in Morristown, New Jersey, where she lived until she died, and Tee was notified— he who then—out of a conspiracy of his own paralyzing guilt and grief and anger, for reasons he thought best left unsaid and unexamined—abandoned, precipitously, his university job, his desk, his books, poetry, all antecedent, and came to live in the enormous isolation of this place.

That memory of the hallway clocks came from the time when Tee used to sleep. Now, instead, past 60, he sat almost all night in his basement kitchen workshop beside the autopsied bodies of laid-out long clocks he moved there from the great hall. Tee didn't know what he was doing as he tinkered

with their catch wheels, their escapements, tracing dates and initials carved into cherry backboards, into ivy, sometimes called larch. Leaning into these coffins each night, he believed that he, too, must hold inside himself a host of inner clocks. Putting his hands into the cool, complicated workings felt like a kind of sleep.

Bone Yard Road, 2016

On a late-October night of arterial lightning surges, the forest floor flooding, thundering, a woman thrown from a car hurtling down a steep lumber road lay stunned for two hours in a heap of wet leaves. She had meant to die. When she came to, she scrambled a long, disoriented way down through the storm-tormented wilderness of a mountainside, where she wandered blindly, without aim, until the trees and brush cleared away and she stumbled in the dark onto an open lawn stretching toward a large house.

When she'd crossed the lawn on hands and knees, and put her shoulder to that first massive door, which creaked ajar with her push, the woman knew only that behind her lay a way she must lose. As other doors gave way, she shouldered them, too, crawling, groping through hallways of lightning migraines, pylons of sodden sedge, carpet, briary thickets, furniture legs, thresholds, lintels where windows streamed with tears and heaven's alien flashes showed her an alert, still forest of owl-faced clocks, a hallway of cricket-minutes chirruping, the ice-gilt tree roots of a suspended chandelier.

She went deeper, further, into the house, and whenever she could, she climbed, taking stairs, her hair and dress dripping. Moments of uncontrollable shivering. Curtained tables, chairs. Clocks. Scrim of cobweb, mothballs, wood smoke, scat, rug tassels, mouse scurry, mold. Hours, years, ages passed inside her as passages, stairwells narrowed, the

way they do in dreams, until finally, crawling, she nudged a door open with her forehead, like a dog or child, and crept onto cool, grouted slabs of a tiled floor, sank toward them, and slept.

She woke to gray light from a small, high window and an oceanic stillness. Beside her, inches from her face, the elegant claw of a porcelain bathtub. Behind her a bright glancing. In a tall heavy mirror leaning against the opposite wall, she saw her body, clay caked red as blood. She turned away.

Much later, she woke again. She pulled herself up beside the tub, smearing mud on the cold white curve of its rim. At first touch the porcelain spigots resisted, shuddered. Nothing. Then a groan from somewhere very deep inside, and a spurt of rusty water. Smell of spoilt eggs. She let the water run, stronger, clearer, cold, then fed in the warmer tap. The drain a rusted, petalled flower. Stripping, she rinsed and rinsed and wrung her own shed dress. She made a drain-stopper of it, lowering herself into the steam. As she did so, the bitter stench of burnt hair. Daylight from the window was captured in the water, and the mirror made the ceiling shift. She pulled two shards of glass from the mats of hair that floated over her shoulders, and set the pieces on the wide rim of the tub. As she did so, she saw in the misted mirror two small handprints.

Who was she? She could or would not remember. Closing her eyes, she slid her head back and down until even the cold tip of her nose slipped beneath the enveloping, natal glass. She dreamt of a bed wedged high in a tree. When she woke she was curled, naked, in the emptied tub bottom, the room growing dark once more.

The Bath Houses, 2000

In late summer, just weeks before the start of fall classes, to be alone after many weeks apart, to escape the call of her work, her husband and daughter, the shop where she etched zinc plates into intaglio prints of peacocks, clouds, strange figures without hands, trapped finches, to get shy of lingering summer students, tasks, everything, Em and Tee had driven a couple hours west to an old bath-house that Em had heard about from a painter friend. "God," she said, as Tee maneuvered his small car down the long weed-rutted lane to a clearing in a pasture, where two white, low circular buildings stood on either side of an old-fashioned well with a bench beside it. The meadows around them were spiked with wildflowers—tickweed, coreopsis, cornflower. "I feel like we're in a Pushkin novel," she said.

One building was the bathhouse for Ladies, the other for Gentlemen, explained a woman in a crisp white, collared blouse and black A-line skirt, seated at a table under a low porch outside the women's pavilion. She explained how the bathhouses were built in Thomas Jefferson's day, and that even Jefferson himself and General Robert E. Lee and his ailing wife had taken the waters here. "Did you bring your swimming suits?" she added, glancing at their empty arms. With a painted fingernail of one age-spotted hand she tapped a metal cash box.

"It's not *strictly* required, you know. But most of our visitors

come from Ivy Hill, and they do wear swimming suits. And bathing caps." Ivy Hill was a nearby resort, an expensive mountain watering hole for lawyers, golfers, and other rich people on vacation or attending corporate conventions and conferences.

Tee admitted that he'd forgotten to bring a suit, and said he would wait outside beside the drinking well. A hand-painted sign claimed that the well water was suitable for consumption and beneficial to human health in many ways, and listed some of them—rheumatism, asthma, digestion—but there was no way Tee was going to let anything from that sulfurous sinkhole touch his lips. He threw himself down on the bench.

But Em was not to be deterred. As she stepped toward the door of the women's bath, the old woman called after her, a bit crossly, "There *are* changing rooms. With curtains. Also paper gowns."

The changing rooms were arranged in cells around the circumference of the round bath-house. There was a skylight in the dome above, and, sure enough, there it was, the apparatus of ramps and gears that had, centuries ago, perhaps lowered the General's wife into the healing sulfurous waters.

For the hour she'd paid for, Em, after dropping her clothes in one of the changing rooms and diving, cleanly into the circle of water, swam slowly, sleekly, through the tea-black, eggy water. As a clutch of women, presumably from Ivy Hill, well corseted in black bathing suits and gold-trimmed bathing caps, earrings dangling, treaded water around one of the ladders and tried not to catch her eye, Em breast-stroked among them, a naiad with ink-stained palms and a strong desire to define her body by whatever it could resist. It was like being in a trance.

After she emerged, refreshed, sulfurous, hair finger-combed and dripping, she'd found a somewhat sulky Tee slouched on the bench where she'd left him, his red hair aflame in the cool afternoon shadow of the little roof pitched over the drinking well.

"You stink," he said. "Good," she said.

"You swam naked."

"Yes. With other women." She refused his jealousy.

They'd wandered off, then, through the adjacent meadow toward an orchard. Behind them they could hear the warbly voice of the desk woman calling after them, "You're really not supposed to, to walk around here like, like that. This is private, this is *private* and *historical* property!"

They had walked right into the sandy rows of the orchard, its furrows pink where the lowering sun struck them, some ladders from the day's picking still propped against the crooked trees, disappearing into blue leafy skirts, rungs to paradise. Ginger-dust. Syrupy light. They held hands, something they could rarely do out in the open air. She sang a nursery song, apples, peaches, pears. Feeling better, Tee sang also, off-key, about a bird that flew, tangled up in blue. He had a terrible voice, but Em loved it. Deep, fruit-perfumed kisses mixed with the egg-tainted bathwater, her hair and collar still wet with it. A breast in his hand. Nipple stippling. Fragments of Spanish spoken somewhere, faint laughing, a pure clang now and then, an engine rumbling, deep within the bladed, diesel-scented, darkening and fragrant aisles.

Though the sun was sinking, bees and wasps pulsed at their feet, grazing split windfalls. As the orchard turned blue, a fringe of taller oaks and beeches beyond its perimeter

blazed with coppery light. Two swallows chased each other above the cuprous crowns of the treetops.

"Look," said T. "The other side of Eden."

"Hmmm," said Em. "Which side are we on, do you think?"

"How can you ask that?"

He was still hurt, testy. They'd argued earlier, in the car, among other things, about why she refused to call him anything but Tee or The Poet, or just Poet. She'd laughed at his real name, Trey Handel, Trey being an old Southern name, apparently, for a son who is the third to bear his grandfather's exact name. "How snooty," she'd said. "How about I call you Drei," she'd said. "Or Thrice. Or Hat Trick. Or 'The Charm.' You know, as in 'third time's the'?"

But he wanted something more from her. Something more personal to him. From her. He wanted her to name him. "How egotistical," she'd said. Usually he was able to convince those upon whom he bestowed nicknames to come up with names for him in return. He was known, for example, by various acquaintances, as, of course, The Monk, but also Byron, The Saint, Dick Handeler, and, by one old girlfriend, Trouble. And now why did she, Em, after swimming naked before strangers in a way that he hadn't dared, have to continue to tease him deliberately by suggesting that they were banished somewhere outside of paradise, rather than proclaiming them as enchanted lovers *inside* its walled garden of peaches, sex, and longing, all that he believed made the two of them special and, he also believed, sheltered and made them different from the rest of the world?

"You know," she said, "Adam didn't need to use all those names he came up with until after he was kicked out of the Garden." But then, "Here," she said, handing him a palmful

of something silky. Where had they come from? What color were they, in the dusk? She pushed his shoulders down. Now, when he stirs at dawn with the taste of peach on his tongue, hands still clutching a cloth or needle-spout can of clock oil, Tee knows he has been, in his sleepless way, dreaming of the secret, unnamable cleft of paradise that was Em.

Bath County, 2016

When the proprietor of Caperton's store first introduced himself to Tee, a decade and a half back, in 2001, Tee had to repeat back what he'd heard. "Debussy?"

Yessir, just like my Daddy, said Billy Caperton.

That had been a wild moment for Tee, freshly and suddenly sprung from the limbo of his stalled life and grief at the University and into this strange, other world that late summer of 2001, beached almost without thought or warning at the lip of an immense expanse of land and house he'd suddenly inherited and which he could only bring himself to colonize minutely, pulling his small Volkswagen Golf, the hatchback holding a few boxes, up to the back entrance of what had once been a kind of English basement kitchen and servants quarters in one of the house's wings, and unloading.

Finally, after a few weeks of living frugally off what he'd brought with him, he ventured forth to buy beer, canned beans, bread, cheese, wending his way back along the way he'd first come, through pine and oak-flushed narrow roads, over creeks scalloped with black falls, past pastures, springs, with Paul Jacobs wrenching Debussy's floaty *Estampes* out of the CD speakers installed in the dashboard, that famished, familiar bodiless flood of ivory, soundboard, and wound strings that touched a yearning in Tee beyond any body (except, he had to admit, the body of Em), evoking ceiling-lifted curtains, all shadow-print and gravel and

hedge-fume of a summer being lived out somewhere else, perpetually.

Every couple of weeks, since that first meeting, Tee had continued to buy his groceries from Caperton, whom he persisted in calling Debussy despite the initial misunderstanding. William "Billy" Caperton had known Tee's family and had been kind, in her long decline, to his increasingly befuddled great-aunt, delivering groceries in his gun-racked pickup out to her among the feral dogs and suspect tenants, and who was a source to Tee, over the ensuing decade, of what had happened to her during those last years at the house. And he had good-naturedly subjected himself on Tee's first visit to the store to an impromptu, intensely urged visit out to the passenger seat of Tee's vehicle to listen to a recording of his namesake on the Golf's CD player.

Why, Tee wondered later, had he been so insistent with Debussy that late morning? Had it been his accumulated solitude and fresh heartbreak that had made him so uncharacteristically pushy, so inappropriate? W.C., a large man, left the Golf door ajar, one laced hunting boot in the gravel as he half-reclined, fidgeting politely on the split leather seat as Tee played for him a dreamy track of *Jardins sous la pluie*, then rather gracefully, for such a big person, extricating himself when a customer finally, thank goodness, arrived with an excuse to release him.

Tee made his bi-weekly foray out for beer and groceries despite the fact that Debussy had over time confided to him that he was working on a cure for cancer and kept his tissue samples and other experimental materials stored in three rusted, padlocked freezer chests out under the detached car-port behind the store. Mrs. Caperton, who worked the

night shift at the regional medical center, and whom Tee had never seen, was somehow implicated, perhaps as supplier or assistant or adjudicator, in these procedures. Capertons was also where Tee picked up what little mail he received, mostly bank and tax statements, utility bills, and various fund and proxy materials from his inheritance that he couldn't fathom and largely ignored. He wrote checks for cash at Capertons when he needed it. "You know," W.C. would say to him in later years, "almost nobody uses checks nowadays. Cash neither. Don't you have a credit card? App on your phone? You could use our ATM." Debussy nodded to a machine beside the door.

Tee tried to time his trips to Capertons, about an hour's drive from home, so as to avoid the late-afternoon clutch of hunters, occasional hikers, and other construction workers and public utility types, men mostly but not all younger than himself, who were always polite enough, a nod of the tractor or camo cap when he pulled up in the faded red Golf, but mildly suspicious, too, even after all this time, of the loner with the short reddish-gray ponytail and thick rectangular eyeglasses. Tee was also careful not to cross paths, if he could help it, with Nura, who was rarely around at midday since most babies, she had once informed him, decided to be born between the hours of 7 AM and 7 PM.

Tee had once spent a strange evening with Nura after some persistent invitations on her part, one winter early on, maybe his first winter at the house. Had she been attracted to him? Did she simply want to help him—his insomnia, his solitude, his dislocation, his depression? Perhaps it was her nature, as a midwife, to sniff out the half-way born, the miscarried, and interfere. Despite her decent whiskey and good moussaka,

her Ornette Coleman and Grateful Dead L.P.s, and all her kind attempts to get Tee to breathe from his diaphragm, to sit correctly, to lie down and let her walk on his spine, the evening had ended badly, with a slightly tipsy Tee going out for a log for the woodstove and simply getting in his car and driving off.

What was it he'd felt afterwards, safely returned down moonless hairpin, tunneling roads to his dim English basement, surrounded by clocks in half-pieces, benches laid with blades, mallets, cog-wheels, drivers, the immense house above him like an uncharted city, imponderable whole of the synecdoche he represented as the heart slamming in his ribcage finally slowed? A sense of his own absurdity, certainly. Of his penis, quiet in his lap. Of Nura, perhaps waking from sour mash doze to discover his cowardly exit.

Truly, what he felt was exquisite relief, as though he'd run a marathon of jeering happy lovers, and lived. He fried three eggs and ate them in the dark with cracked pepper and Tabasco. Keying open a warm bottle of Guinness from the countertop, he stood, lit by the glacial, neon glow of the refrigerator whose contents he surveyed, and took a long, thirsty swallow. Calmed at last, he settled down to his stool, his waiting tools. "To be awake is to be alive," Thoreau had said. Well, solitude is 100-proof, Tee replied, as though in conversation with the fawn-like first light of day touching the grimed windows. It magnifies. Intoxicates. A brutal sublime.

Nura abided in her kindness to Tee afterwards, was the better person, even touching his arm now and then when they ran into one another at the store, pushing little hand-sewn mesh packets of Valerian and other roots and herbs into his hands, remedies for the sleeplessness and the melancholy she

made Tee himself aware of, an aura he wore like the stench of a gutted deer or a mothballed suit jacket. But his shame in the wake of his behavior with her only made him even more restrained and awkward in her presence afterwards than he already was by nature, and he always slipped away when he encountered her, as soon as he could.

A dusty bell tied with string to the door-springs jangled when Tee entered. It was always dirty in Capertons, and the late morning October light fell in nostalgic, cinnamon-moted stripes along the low counter, the cash register. It took Tee a moment to adjust to the dim room. Nura was at the counter, as it turned out (had she come on foot across the orchard, Tee wondered? He hadn't seen her van in the lot), describing to Debussy with much gesticulation the breech birth she'd attended for the past 32 hours at an A-frame up in Lacy Hollow. Her maroon yoga pants and felted wool Birkenstocks looked wet and splotchy—certainly that couldn't be blood and other birth effluvia, Tee thought, surely she changed clothes afterwards? Or wore protective booties? More likely it was moisture from the drenched pastures. Sometimes his own fastidiousness appalled him.

A pea-sized pearl of spittle wobbled at the corner of her mouth as, between sips of Debussy's bad burnt coffee, Nura replayed the mother's discomfort, her agony, the fainting partner, the tricky gymnastics and maneuverings of breech and crowning at dawn. "Interesting," said Debussy, shooting Tee a companionable glance and beginning to stoke a cardboard box with the things he knew Tee had come for. Tee nodded and ducked into one of the store's two aisles to peruse the canned vegetables, noticing as he did so a large, sweating plastic bucket on the floor at Nura's feet, partly pushed

behind the counter. He sometimes wondered if Nura, too, were somehow complicit in Debussy's scientific activities.

Debussy in quick order had Tee's two boxes of olive oil, potatoes, canned tomatoes, oatmeal, wedge of cheddar cheese, loaves of bread, two cartons of eggs, bundle of greens, and a case of stout waiting for him, topped with two thick Sunday newspapers that he'd collected for him over the weeks, and a small stack of mail bundled with a rubber band. Tee paid up, shouldered the boxes, and was outside juggling with the Volkswagen's hatch when he sensed Nura beside him. "Here you go," she said, tucking something into the front pocket of his plaid shirt. "Something for the colder weather, home grown." She lightly squeezed his arm. And then she turned, heading off for the fields behind Capertons, and the sprawling apple orchard that lay between the store and her own small house. Without the white bucket, Tee noticed, also noting her rope of pewter braid, a pendulum swinging along her back, and her soft rear-end moving with suppleness beneath those yoga pants. Middle age. If Nura could be, then so must he be, too, he who went for days without speaking out loud, like someone already very much older than he actually was.

Tee was halfway home when he remembered Nura and patted his pocket. Three big, fragrant joints wrapped in homemade papers. Tee snorted. It had been years. He had to pull off the road a bit—there wasn't much of a shoulder anywhere—to dig for matches in the glove box. By the time he'd turned into the stone pillars of his long driveway, shawled by Virginia creeper, crimson now, and grapevine, he was as high as a hawk. Was he at last watching his own ridiculous shadow from a great height, the little boxy hatchback veering off now toward The Hole under cover of the alley of kudzu-flocked

oaks and boxwoods? Neil Young had replaced Bach on the box—was Tee the last person on earth with a CD player in his car? Someone at Capertons had said they were about to stop doing that, everything was moving to Bluetooth and streaming, whatever that meant—wailing about a dead blind man on the side of the road, eyes eternally opened to the sky.

The Nursery, 2016

Wait, thinks the woman who'd catapulted from a car and who had found her way down the side of a thickly wooded mountain and into a big, strange house. Go more slowly. The knob is glass in her fist and the door opens into a long, dim, yellow room. Who is she, at this threshold? The ceiling high, then steeply slanting, cut with four deep dormers. Filthy draperies, thick with cobwebs. Window seats built in there. At the far end, a dazzling corner of windows, a conservatory. Inside the room now, moving toward the light. Passing a whitewashed fireplace, its black, ashen mouth. Passing under a chandelier, prisms swagged with cobwebs. A gothic crib. Two iron day beds, sheeted chairs. Shelves. Picture books in heaps. A grime-shellacked cup. Oddly, a red plastic bong, clogged with resin. Butterflies pinned to cotton under three black-framed panes. Lapis powder still on their wings, each like a stained glass ear.

She listens.

Bright wind in the putty, the glassy casements. On hands and knees in the sun-room now. Vulture and cloud-shadow on her arms. Then stale ginger cookies from a cardboard box in a cupboard of a little kitchen nook. Ravenous fairy tale swellings on the tongue. Mealy. Another bathtub, another groaning summons of water, for hours steeping in the sulfurous tea, the girdle of lesions on her calves and ankles burning. Awaking in the dark, skin natal, withered. Someone's

robe on a peg, splayed with faded blossoms. She puts her arms through its sleeves and wraps it around her own naked body. Then she drags one of the small beds beneath the glass roof, where, under an unkempt blur of stars, she falls again, like a child who must dream something essential to her survival.

Bat in the House, 2016

A frosty morning in late October and the woodstove was already cranked at Capertons. Climbing up the front steps, Tee glanced at the "Dump Trump" and "Say NO to Hillary" signs taped in the small front window. He sniffed, wondered if this show of non-partisanship earned the ever-mystifying Debussy any new friends in these parts. Deeply apolitical, even Tee cared enough to hope the blathering hothead wouldn't win.

Time to get that ancient oak felled by lightning during the recent storms sawed and stacked, thought Tee, who supplemented his oil furnace with wood heat in the winter months. The store was always heated with wood. While waiting for Debussy to load his empty boxes, Tee stood at the counter grazing through one of his stockpiled newspapers, listening to the men talking and warming their hands at the tin lizzie. Deer season had started, and the men were cumbersome in camo vests and caps. Boots. Old Duck was poking his blunt pointer finger at his cell phone, but the others were listening to Vernon Lacy.

"I can tell you for sure theys such such a thing as PMS," Vernon was saying. "It's real." "That so?" said somebody. "Well," Vernon continued, "Debbie started to crying, and she just couldn't stop. I begged her to quit. Two days of it. Even when Little Morris shook her. Her daddy come to take her over to the hospital. I took the kids to mama's. She's just come back

home now. But I knew what it was. That's right." The men murmured their sympathy. A log shifted in the stove.

Their conversation moved on to what Maggie Shifflett had seen one night the past week, working late in the nearby garage where she had a small upholstery business. The yards in the little cluster of houses and double-wides that surrounded the store were dark, and what did she see but a large female in a white dress running hard up the back alley. Frightened for the woman, Maggie had dialed 911. Turned out it was no woman, but Greg Stannup, married father of two, deacon in the Lacy Hollow Baptist church, wearing a woman's nightgown, clutching a paper grocery sack of women's underwear. Seemed it was he who'd been stealing women's brassieres and slips and underthings off clotheslines all fall. Duck, texting, looked up from his lit palm. "I'll be," Duck said. Again the men shook their heads.

Tee, back on the road, was pretty sure the men at Capertons thought he was gay. They always nodded to him, or he'd say how's it going and they'd say okay I guess or can't complain, and look away. Well, no matter. They would be right not to think of him at all, oldish and owlish and odd as he was, with insomnia's dark circles under his eyes. Right now he was thinking about the metallic tissue of the cannon, hour, and minute wheels of one of his Victorian long clocks. Because Tee didn't really know what he was doing when he fiddled around inside these intricate, jeweled wildernesses of cogged wheels and pallets and dead-beat escapements, of crutches and cocks and pendulums, consulting various manuals sporadically and most of the time winging it, he felt utterly free to be wrong and took the same sad pleasure both in failing to discover a fault as in finding one, as he thought he perhaps

had, sometime in the early hours of the morning. A broken metal tooth, it seems, had been held in place by a thin flap of metal so that it was capable of leaning over, undetected, and jamming the works. He had stumbled upon this by completely removing the wheel.

He was eager to get back to the opened case—he'd cleaned and oiled the hour and minute pipes and laid them out—but he would have to get that wood cut up soon. Maybe later today. He might seem like a girlie man, the thick black glasses frames he'd always worn, and the ridiculous ponytail he couldn't bring himself to chop off, mostly because he was almost completely bald now, on top, but he was strong. What would those men at the store think if they knew he'd once been a college professor and had written and even published poetry? All that walking on the mountain kept him fit. He could see his breath in the air. The car's heater had been busted for years. He slipped a Bartok CD into the player. Then changed his mind and put in Nick Drake.

Just past the stretch of orchard behind the store, he saw Nura. For some reason he had not come up with a moniker for her, perhaps out of guilt for his bad behavior. She was wearing a long purple skirt and barn coat, waving from the drive below her white cottage. She had seen his car, and was gesturing frantically for him to stop, to come up. He'd already passed her mailbox and was tempted to keep going. Pretend he hadn't seen her. Windshield fogged by frost. Sunglare. That certain slant of light.

She met him beside her van parked in the small gravel plot of her driveway. He'd never seen her crying before.

"We could really use your help," she managed to say, out of breath, her voice with its wavery contralto, usually

so calm, dragging him by the sleeve up the rock-strewn hill and through a metal cattle-guard toward her steps and front door. "So glad you were passing at just this moment."

We? Tee wondered. At the door, she put a hand on his arm. She was shivering. "Go in very carefully," she said. "It's, it's flippy flopping all around the room. Could be rabid."

That spittle again, at the corners of her mouth. Nura was agitated. "Here," she said, "take this." She handed him a long-handled broom. "And this." The bucket he'd seen before.

Tee nodded with what he hoped looked like sturdy sympathy and not the impatience he was feeling. He went in. Jeez. Just a bat. They were coming in this time of year, down the chimneys. He'd caught and released two himself in the past couple of weeks.

The room was dim, no lights on, but without turning his head much, he registered a small figure cowering on Nura's couch in a kimono or caftan of some kind. Whimpering sounds from there, and Nura's anxious quavering behind him from the porch telling him to be careful.

The bat was hanging beside a low window frame. Tee put down the broom and took off his flannel shirt. He moved quickly, covering the winged and hapless mammal with the garment, careful not to pinch. He wrapped and dropped the wad into the bucket. Passing by the couch, eyes better adjusted now, he could see a woman, hands and feet tied with colored scarves, the kimono partly open. Tee kept moving.

"I'll take care of this," he said to Nura, back out on the porch. Nodding back to the living room, he said, "everything okay in there?" Nura's face flushed but she didn't avert her gaze. "It's, well, it's just what it looks like. Ah, you know. We

were just. And then. Skylar is *deathly* afraid of bats. So thank you, Tee, thank you, thank you so much."

He could feel Nura watching him, shirtless, as he loaded the bucket into the hatch of the Golf. "I'll leave this for you to pick up later at the store," Tee said, nodding at the bucket. Was she grateful or mocking, Tee wondered. He glanced down at his white chest hairs. Embarrassed or...defiant? Embarrassed himself, he recalled his French exit from Nura's place all those years ago. He found it hard to read people these days. Shifting the car into reverse, he made his escape.

from The Refrigeration Series *[Em's Notebook],*
c. 2000

Tee wasn't proud of this, but angry and helpless in the wake of her departure and unable to overcome his jealousy not so much of Em's family and her work but of her success, he had stolen her notebooks after she'd left town. He still had a key to the print shop, and had simply gone in and taken the journals from her office. He was, at first, most interested in the pages about himself or in any details the pages might reveal about her husband Paul and her daughter. But as Tee found himself rifling through the notebooks on sleepless nights in his apartment, he was overcome not only by her clear gratitude to and love for him, but by the reach and openness of her curiosity, especially in light of the challenges of her marriage. She actually seemed *grateful* to him, to Tee himself. Accustomed to her teasing and her unsparing frankness with him, he had not expected this, and it moved him in his grief.

Paul left at last this morning, taking M. and one of her girlfriends. The girls to stay with his parents. I breathe again by late afternoon. I still haven't told him that I found his scrapped letter & taped it together (cf. Mme. Heger finding and stitching back together C. Brontë's love letter to her husband, those orthopedic sutures, C's floral blue, desperate, perfect and ardent French torn carelessly by Heger and tossed into a bin, <u>but not before he scribbled a shoemaker's address in the margin</u>). Well, Paul's "person" is no Brontë. Secretary, maybe? colleague? His <u>ridiculous</u> scrawl

to her, "Don't worry about me, I'm used to being abandoned" &c. Good luck, sweetheart, whoever you are, is what I say. Mr. Paul Pitiful. Always the victim.

Tee reminding me later about Dickinson's Master Letters. Love letters. Angry. V. erotic. Letters ever meant to be sent? read? discovered by one's wife as she's emptying the trash?
Washed the bedsheets 2X. Thrice.

Walking Sumac Trails along the river with Tee found an old refrigerator dumped upstream, now wedged in the shallows among slick roots and vines. The door long gone, hinges rust-red, upright against the bright blue sky, little stiff flags, arrow-heads. Inside: the rotted, gently bobbing capsized carapace of a pond slider. Its bottom shell, slimed with mosses, so lovely, yellowed like a skull fretted with knitted fontanel, tectonic plates... an abandoned house within an abandoned house, T. said.

T. is my Brother Orphan.

He fished out the shell for me and carried it back to the studio in the back of his car. Drying on a windowsill here now beside antler horn, three cicada husks, a cracked yellow water pistol silted with mud, a dried stalk of Russian sage Tee brought to me early on, a "cure for melancholy" he sd.

Buy: soy yogurt. ~~Excedrin~~. Cremant.

The Glass Room, 2016

Whatever dark river or lightning strike or bad choice or accident made and undid her, whether or not she was the author of her own tale, whether it was a story terrifying, melancholy, dull, or full of delight, danger, abuse, and of losses few or innumerable, the woman who had crawled out of Orphan Mountain and, unbeknownst, into Trey Handel's house did not belong to those forces now. She was secreted in another kind of story, high as a tower, where through the roof of a glass room she watched the clock of the world pass over her—tart, persimmon yellow equinoctial sun, unbuttoned blouses of cloud, cerulean byways, star clots, the constellations in their leg-irons, the moon in its guises, mysterious silks of the galaxies—and she moved, sometimes without clothing, through urns of light and passages of darkness, and slept in a bed with rails like a baby or a crone and fed a scratch of cracker meal to birds who visited at a wide sill of the one leaded window she could crank open.

Below her the woods burned, a piazza and fountain, and beyond that, leaf-flames girdling a black pond scoured by regal swaths of the geese who fell into their own reflections, then lifted off again with strange, concussive, mournful bellows, departing in Vs that reflected those they left in their wake when they swam across the dark water. Sometimes the man with the gray ponytail, reddish in the sun, and black glasses walked among them, shouldering an axe.

Up here, safe, her wounds slowly healed in warm, rank baths she drew and emerged from, silver hair untangling in lengthening rivulets down her shoulders, back. She felt like someone very old who has outlived everyone she might have harmed or who might have harmed or loved her. Anyone she might have loved. When she saw herself in a window, a mirror—dark eyes, filmy hair, loose belly, starred sloop of breasts—she opened her mouth in a cloud of mist against the glass as though to practice making a word. Or name. Occasionally a mouse scampered, quick, along the moldings. A clubhouse smell, fecal pellets in the drawers among beeswax candle stubs. On cold nights she wore the robe, burned with matches from a drawer old chair rails, papers, boxes, in the sooty maw of a fireplace. She ate all the old food leftover in the cupboards, thought about the man below, and whether he would ever enter this room, or if she would ever leave it.

from The ~~Refrigeration~~ Incarnation Series
[Em's Notebook], c. 2000

Icebox as heart. (who says "icebox" anymore?))

<u>Idea for series:</u> *show up with Polaroid camera and ask random people if I can photograph the unedited contents of their refrigerators.*

Premonition: <u>joy lurks inside me.</u>

<u>Starting with my own:</u> *Missionary position condo fridge, rectangular box, scoured inside with cleanser & inhuman light. Aura of emptiness. Metal grill shelving. A feeling of transience—a beach house vibe. Clean upon exit or pay the security deposit. Paul's is the top shelf, which he stocks himself when he's in town: fake-O yogurt (pudding cups). Hot dogs. bananas. (why all the phallic foods? &... why refrigerate bananas?) Diet drinks. <u>My shelf:</u> bagged lettuce. Tofu from a local commune wrapped in wax paper. Three bottles of white German wine. In a bin: net bag of onions, baggie of tarragon. Much re-used cardboard carton half-full of eggs from Johanna's hens. Can't see the half-full part because the carton is closed. Jug of water. Freezer: a sad geode of frost.*

Visitors to Wm Blake's Lambeth cottage describe his small rooms, a maze strung with clotheslines of drying prints, bread husks used to wipe ink from the copper plates. His pants worn shiny (as a machinist's). When they were actually wearing clothes, he and his helpmeet Katherine, Catherine?, (illiterate wife. Apocryphal—the

illiterate part?) who enjoyed sitting naked in their garden (also apocryphal?). A post-lapsarian atelier.

<u>****call Art Korner:*</u> *order paper for intro & advanced classes (Hahnemüle?); ink; buff kitakata. Syllabus.*****

Poet brought to the studio the Amherst College Press facsimile portfolio of the ED Master Letters.

I love the inkblots, foxed, embossed creased writing papers, her wild, briary, storm-slanted script. Palpable pain. Cross-hatched words and plus-mark variants (e.g., I cannot talk any more tonight, I cannot stay any longer tonight now, I cannot stay any longer tonight). I almost wrote "any lover" tonight. Which? All? I have not told Tee about my series; don't want him to clean up his kitchen before I show up to shoot.

Tee's Apartment, 2001

A*n Horologist's Book of Hours*. Em had not liked the title when Tee first showed up at the print shop a year ago with his poetry manuscript. Largely in response to his almost instantaneous infatuation with her and with the way that she, a stranger, had immediately and openly disagreed with his choice, Tee had changed the title of his collection to simply *Our Hour*. And at last, months and months later, the book had come, fresh from the printer, a box of ten author's copies, and on the cover of each the title, *Our Hour*, by Trey Handel III, and that wild detail from the fifth in Em's trapped bird series. In it, a red man floated in the opening of a flagstone impost of an old castle window, as in a clouded sea or sky. His arms were held straight out, his body making a crux and his eyes closed. His wrists bristled with white timepieces and his closed eyelids and cock are indigo. Then we see that all of this—the window, space, man, are held in the eye of a large yellow bird, whose pupil and iris almost fill the page, with just a hint of gold beak, an implied nimbus of candent wings.

They had been celebrating, and Em was asleep on his mattress, naked except for her green skirt, bunched up around her waist and two gold earrings, one in each lobe. On her side, fetal, she held the gathered fabric in her arms like a blanket. A fly lazily grazed the lips of two empty bottles of champagne. Her hair was silvering at the temples. A few glints in her pubic hair as well, he'd noticed.

He wouldn't lie to himself—he had loved it when, earlier, she had held the book and read aloud from it when he was behind and inside her (I like it this way, she'd once said—we're both looking in the same direction). Behind her, he could see the page, too, though he was on his knees, his eyes closed as the poem grew within her. His words swelled, filling her throat, his, her head, his, hers. And then the book hitting the wall where she'd flung it, convulsing. Her cries were his own then. Later, as she slept, he realized that she'd been unable to read the poem's final stanza before she came and came and came. At one time that might have bothered him, he admitted. It did not. *We* finished the poem, he thought. Fucking, better than words.

Somewhere a lawn mower. Surf of the street below. Em was snoring now, so much noise emitting from such a tiny body, Tee thought. He felt almost brotherly toward her in such moments. How unlikely, how strangely perfect, that they were both orphans, would never have to go through what their friends would face, some were already facing, with their aging parents, nursing homes, dementia, protracted dotage with its inconvenient, expensive, and exponential indignities, burying the awful along with the sentiment. What they had was nothing but strange, idealized projections, fragmented memories, and inchoate longings. Perhaps that explained, in part, their bond. He liked thinking of them facing a future together. Though he had to confess that he wished she wasn't married. With a teenage child, no less.

A spindle of drool had pooled at the canthus of Em's full, pink mouth. He licked, then sucked it. He loved her crooked teeth, and tongued them until she woke.

from The Incarnation Series *[Em's Notebook]*, c. 2000

<u>The Poet's refrigerator:</u> *O sensuous Eremite! Small, under the counter, as in a European kitchen. Or a dorm. Package of Swedish flatbread. Five flat sheets of Maine salmon, one ripped open and obviously gnawed. Strong smell of the sea. Plastic pitcher of iced coffee or some other brown liquid. Carton of Heavy Cream (forcible stench of blue mold). Two bottles left in a damp cardboard six pack of Pilsner Urquel. Pie slice of brie. Also gnawed—teeth marks (remember <u>teethmarks</u>) (does he own a fork and knife? does he eat standing up?). Three green apples. Bottle of Aloe Vera juice, crusted at the screwcap. Old lettuce leaves decoupaged to the floor sill, just under the closed produce bin, cloudy with obscure reddish vegetable matter (beet tops?). In the freezer, a frosty half gallon of gin and a package of frozen peas (used, apparently, to ice down sprains).*

Sprains from . . . our Vine & Trellis sutra???).
<u>New idea: Focus on restaurants/bars, all within a one-mile radius of the campus:</u>

The Angus Corral

Pig Heaven BBQ

L'Escargot

The Derry Aire

—>*The way the "personal" might complicate the project in the wrong way. Explore the disconnect between "health codes" / storefront and "reality" What do you show to the public and what is the truth (the dark and lonely offices of the trash bin)? The ferocity of limits, of obstruction. The surprise of it (I'm here to photograph your excavated soul!) too violent maybe for friends? (for me?) (protecting T.). <u>Leave friends / The Poet out of it.</u> These photographs will become the matrix/seedbed for the prints, which will show me, as I always hope, the questions I need to ask.*

The Hole, 2016

The woman Tee finally found hidden in the attic of his house now lifts her breath-taking face to him. She is older, like him, lines around the mouth, the eyes. But she is beautiful, gaunt oval face, violet eyes, pale hair threaded with faint strawberry ample about her shoulders. When Tee looks at her, he sees her as a girl. He sees her very old. He sees Em. Could it be her?

But no: this woman has very different eyes. Em's were bright and gray as kindled coals. These are violet eyes. And different hands. How well he remembered Em's, small and deft hands, circling his cock. Or cleanly drawing a line into a plate of zinc. They would not be these hands, the hands of the mystery woman, large and unmarked but for the residual, thready scabs of her struggle through the accident and storm that had brought her to this house. But she does not tell him about the accident, or what preceded it. Perhaps she cannot.

Tell me again the story of how you found me, she says. He has trouble looking at her for too long. She shimmers. Won't hold still in his eyes. Could he be hallucinating her?

Memory is flawed, and secret-keeping terribly perfected, and yet each morning this past week there has been the astounding surprise of her, awake at the table in his small kitchen, plank of hair between the shoulders of the robe, its faded pattern of cerulean bridges, sakura branches, another world. And even more incredible, the astonishment of his

having actually been *asleep*, as though dreaming was what he must do in order to wake again and find her real.

Hard to know how to begin when she asks him this. He wants to get it right when he repeats it to her, even though it's only been a few days, no more than a week. He's lost track. So much slippage everywhere. Perhaps if he can narrate this to her, she can tell him how she came to him, and why.

What had tipped him off? Had it been the occasional groan in the house of distant pipes, drainings, flushings, like an organ heard from a great distance, as over water from a remote village fair? An unusual blur of chimney smoke over the house? Or that evening in late November, when, coming back from his walk, having smoked some of Nura's pot, he'd looked up for no reason at the high, conservatory, perched at the western end of the old nursery wing, and thought he'd hallucinated a figure pressed there, at the very pane, naked, arms stretched in a V, legs akimbo, pale pubic tuft, limbs, wild hair hatched with the solstice light of Sagittarius?

The truth was he looked up one morning after a long night of working on a clock, ribs sore from leaning in, more tired and hungry than he had been in a long time. Instead of walking to the stove, though, he began wandering through the whitewashed tunnels of the cellar, finding himself eventually at the foot of a flight of narrow, cupboarded stairs that led up to the large pantry of the house kitchen proper. Nothing much left there—empty shelves, canning jars, some large pans hanging from hooks, empty hooks, nesting pots, webs. In the kitchen, deep, vacant sinks, lonely spigots, an old pump and trough. An ocean-liner of a cook stove, huge ovens, several stained chopping blocks. He must, as a child, have spent time here on visits, just as he must once have

slept in the dormered upstairs nursery wing, which may account for how, by instinct, he, climbing, climbing, found it again, found her, huddled in a child's bed in the center of the sunroom in weak December light, wrapped in a filthy quilt. Please, she said, opening her fractured, amethyst eyes.

Eggs with cheese. Salsa from a jar. Black beans sautéed with red onions. Cider. Rye bread. She'd vomited that night, bending on the door stoop in the square of freezing porch light. Then, stripping sheets, Tee remade the bed for her in his own small room, the baseboard heater ticking in there, to warm it. He'd been silent as she stood, after showering, in the doorway in a pair of his pants and a thermal shirt, watching him, hair wet, lank. Her clavicles like two shining keys. He stood out of her way, and she lay down. Later, on the futon in his workshop, where he tried to rest instead of working, fearing he might keep her awake with his muttering among the clocks, he knew he should be wild with wonder and worry—who is she, where did she come from, why is she here, who is looking for her, is she dangerous, what is wrong with her, what should I do with her, how can I help her, how can I protect myself. Why was he always afraid? He'd asked her, several times, to explain, to at least give her name, but she just shook her head, not sorrowfully, exactly, not vacantly or stupidly, but with a gesture that refused explanation—and, even more frightening to him, would she leave? And yet, surprisingly, for the first time in many, many years, he could not keep his eyes open, falling instantly into a profound, almost enchanted sleep.

It was not until the next morning, just before waking, that he dreamed for the first time in a long time the dream of Em that he used to have almost every morning after they parted

that horrible afternoon in his apartment, the dream of coming upon, in a dense fabular forest, a cottage made of glass. The windows are steamed, sulfurous. Icicles shackle the roof like candy icing. He knows Em is inside. He puts his mouth to the pane. It's me, Emma, it's me, he whispers. Emma, Em, Em. I'm here. Black strokings from inside, the squeaking pad of a palm swiping the mist aside, revealing two hothouse, unclothed bodies, knotted together, glistening. How could you do this to me, Emma, he cries, it's me, it's me. The bodies fall apart, and then it's just one body, and the face gazing back at him, implacably, impassively, from within the sugar house of ice, is, at first, the face of a little girl. Then it is his own.

Is it possible that he has really slept so much these past several nights? It has been snowing lightly for two days, the windows swathed, flocculent with white. Not enough snow yet, though, to have to attach the plough to his little John Deere, he decides. He looks across the table. She is still there, waiting for him to speak, to tell the story of her rescue. Her face opens to him, the gift of it. A white sickle scar on her front tooth. Her eyes unfathomable, restless, like lilac ocean surf, creased at the edges, her spindrift, ephemeral skin. She seems on the verge of disappearing. Don't go, he wants to say.

Earlier, she had made up a fresh fire in the wood stove. "There is coffee," she said.

How did she know how to lay such a fine fire? When was the last time someone made coffee for him? They do not touch. They walk around each other, a kind of dance.

But it is as though they have always lived here together, he thinks. He hasn't slept this much in decades, there on the futon opened up at the back wall of the shop beside the

small enameled woodstove. He has given her his bedroom, with the electric heat, the mattress. He rubs his eyes, pours a cup, and sits across from her. Her hands are busy now, as she waits.

"What's that you're making?"

"A bracelet."

He sees that she has found some bits from the boxes, drawers, in his shop, maybe pilfered the old, long library card catalog drawer he uses for storage: a pile of mismatched wrist-watch parts—flat disks, enameled faces with their circlets of numerals, pine needle-like arrows, hour and minute, sun and moon details, cogwheels, metal links—some wire. Pliers. Shears. Did she move about the room while he slept? Did she look at him while he dreamed of Em? Her fingertips are raw, the backs of her long, large hands a fading welter of healings, a delta of blue veins.

"Maybe I should try to get out today," he says, washing his mug out at the sink. "Visit the store."

She goes to the window. Emma steps to the window. Wipes it. It's me, it's me. He must still be asleep. "I think maybe wait until the snow stops." Whose voice saying that? Em's? The Woman's? His own?

The large white wall calendar, hung on its nail. Grid of numbers. Winter solstice.

The shortest day of the year.

Who are you? he wants to ask.

"It's my birthday," he says instead.

The Award, 2001

They had been sitting upright, legs wrapped around each other, foreheads pressed together on his bed, which was the height of the sill of the opened window. There had been recent rain and three pink blossoms were stuck to the screen. Sweat cooling. It was afterwards, and he was still inside her. Was this the peace of the meditators, the quiet contemplatives, his friends who were religious or who practiced yoga, he wondered, he who could never seem to believe, to clear his mind, try as he might. Yet here he was, as though waking suddenly to discover that he'd been, for quite a while, blissful, worshipful, beside himself. Relieved was what he was, mostly, especially after this past year, the tenure hurdle at work (he'd gotten through it, but he'd wished his teaching evaluations had been stronger—"Mr. H is aloof" or "Tee seems to care more about making us love what he likes than in helping us with our poems" or, worse, "Mr. Handel should never wear sandals") (a kind of mocking doggerel scrawled across the bottom of the comment form).

And then the wish that his book had done better, gotten more notice. He'd been angry that its beauty, its originality, had not been noticed by someone important, especially since he, Tee, was not temperamentally suited to toting the book around and pushing it on others at public readings and writing conferences. Or to "blogging" about it, which was suddenly *de rigeur*. He sensed that his editor was a bit

miffed about his passivity, and Tee worried about the next manuscript. Would Roger take it? Would there even be a next book? Maybe he should write a memoir. Those were all the rage. Yes, he would do that. A memoir would be a success. But what did he have to say?

He hadn't written much poetry lately, maybe two poems in all of the past year. He reassured himself that this was normal in the tenure cycle amidst the stress of gathering all of those documents proving one's worth and then subjecting them to the scrutiny of his peers. Not to mention the teaching, committee work, getting the first book out. These tensions were harder to care about and bear the more marginalized they became in his psychic landscape, his head and heart now obsessively flooded with Em, his desire for her, protecting her devotion to him, his addiction to her loveliness, her body, his wish to be with her always, his jealousies, he couldn't help them—her successful shows, the glowing reviews of them—in the *Times*, for God's sake, *Artforum*, and the fucking *New Yorker*.

Perhaps hardest to take were the separations, trips she made to New York galleries with her devoted students, trips to and from DC with her daughter to see Paul, out of town to visit his family. That trip abroad to the Italian artist's community. Her work. Her work. Her work. It took so much time. The print shop where lately she'd been making exquisite woodcuts, women crouched in the slatted shadows of large upside-down baskets. She'd been adding metals to the prints—gold leaf pressings, glinty fletches in the wicker. Each print she showed Tee ripped through his ribs, they were so lush and so lovely.

Instead of using the time when he was forced to be apart from Em to work, or to see his friends, he'd more and more cut

himself off—from the Department, the gym where he sometimes played a round of basketball with some other junior faculty, the occasional lunch or coffee with a colleague. And of course he had no family except the aged, crazy great-aunt by marriage, living off in the boonies. Instead, he listened to his records, walked a lot, and felt very sorry for himself.

"I have something to tell you," Em was saying (a little warily?, he thought), sitting back, wiping her forehead, eyes silver, onyx lashes, flicker of his own miniscule face and torso mirrored twice, once in each pupil. She blew on his face.

He felt himself slip out of her, saw the imprint of his own forehead, red patch, flushed bindi on her own. Semen puddle on the sheet.

Silence. Then, clearing her throat,

"It seems I've won a Dover."

A beat.

"A Dover?"

"I just found out. They called to tell me. At school."

This was a lie; she'd really heard a few days ago, but had been waiting for the right time to tell him.

Just found out? Tee was scrambling now, his slowed pulse now racing. Dover, Dover. The Dover. This was one of those big awards —five years, no teaching. A genius grant. Can't apply for it. Have to be nominated. Lots of money for it, can't teach while you have it.

He snorted before he could collect himself. By then Em was already standing, moving to the door, flushed, poking buttons at buttonholes, twitching her skirt into place, grabbing up her bag, pushing her feet into her shoes.

"I knew you'd react this way," she said. "It's why I didn't want to tell you."

Tee was paralyzed with remorse, legs akimbo, abandoned on the bed. He closed his mouth. "What way," he said.

"The genius part. You're the genius. I'm just a diddler in acids."

"Emma!" he'd said, "Emma, Emma, Em. Emma!," rising off the bed now, crossing the room, holding her against his hammering chest, excuses flooding out of him, his response: just surprise, the suddenness of the news. He praised her, razzed her about being deemed a genius, calling her Curie, Einstein, Aristotle (but really, he was thinking, a "genius"? talented, true, and though she fucked like a goddess, the woman could barely balance a checkbook), and she'd stayed a long while in his arms, reassuring him that nothing would change, she'd still work in the shop, would not be leaving town, that maybe she could use some of the money for him, for them, a book collaboration, maybe a trip they could manage to take somewhere together.

They'd parted on the apartment landing as the lovers they were. But his own heart resisted her news wildly all night, rapidly, weirdly, and he couldn't sleep. And by the time Em reached her car, she was crying so hard she had to sit on the curb, holding her knees and rocking, as kids from the complex passed by on their skateboards, bicycles, staring, and the pole lamps eventually came on with a electrical crackle overhead.

New Year's Day, 2017

The woman blown in by the storm was asleep in Tee's bed. He stood in the doorway. Almost without breathing, it seemed, she lay motionless on his sheets, her face—so weathered, so strangely natal—a white heart against the slate pillowcase. Her eyelids twitched, amethyst in the shadows. Was she dreaming? Of what?

Tee almost got lost making his way again back up to the attic rooms where he'd first discovered her. He was looking for something to wake him from this dream. To make sense. Reveal who she was.

What he found: a tangle of brassiere and torn dress stained red with mud, wrung like a dish rag and dried at the foot of an old bathtub. Sharp slivers of glass—windshield? bottle? not weathered enough for sea—lined up like a shell collection along its wide rim. Long light hairs everywhere, tub, cot, floating in air. A nest of blankets, pair of panties, one mud-caked leather shoe, again seemingly stepped out of wet and left to dry in a dormer like the shed body of a soul taken up precipitously into the rapture.

In the nursery's galley kitchen, empty cracker boxes, paper cookie wrappers, overturned rice tins, perhaps left by some of his great-aunt's tenants or the crew that stayed there a while to clean up the place before he arrived—what she'd been living on. The fireplace a charred maw, half-burned dismantled furniture, shelving, a wrecked desk drawer. Flame-bitten

spines of books. Had she burned them to stay warm? Another pile of children's books, intact, beside the trundle bed in the glass room. It had been a long time since he'd lowered his torso that far to rest in such a place, perching gingerly on the edge of the thin mattress, and opening the book at the top of the tall stack, a page verdant, nocturnal, and green ushered him suddenly into a lost, familiar room, "good night to the old lady," he read aloud, "whispering 'hush.'" No gun beneath the pillow, no knife in a cupboard, no wallet or purse, no scrap of illuminating or identifying paper. No little white mouse to find in this picture, no clue, crouched behind the clock, beside the hearth. No diary, letter, ransom note, address book.

She'd clearly survived up here for a while, as much as a month, maybe longer. Well, he supposed he would have to go in to the store, see if anyone was talking about anything—an accident on the interstate, runaway lover, lost camper or hiker, domestic trouble, that sort of thing. He had no internet or cell connection out here. He felt glad about that. Bought him some time.

Tee stood and walked to the window. Only the towering oaks still held their leaves, and he could see past Orphan Mountain, its low swell, all the way to the most distant pale blue ridges, some deep snow already fallen there, the nearer bronze leaves dredging the pond, patches of recent snow, and the stiff green brushes of the evergreens, a reddish, hormonal light suffused in the expanse of forest.

He stepped back. On the cold glass, prints—fingertips, flat palms, breasts? Tongue? Is this where she'd stood, naked, the November day he'd seen her from the ridge? He adjusted his eyes again. Stepped up and breathed on the cold glass.

Pictures? Something like writing, backwards, cursive, the way Blake, Em once told him, taught himself to write in reverse on the copper plates so his *Songs* could be read correctly when printed. "I wander through each chartered street," &c.

Hard to make out the scrawl and loops—Jules? June. Duke. Juke, maybe. Yes, J-U-K-E. *Juke*. Whatever that meant. Juke it was. Juke held. *Juke Was Here.* He would call her Juke. No, no. No. He would *ask* her if he might, if he could have her permission, the privilege, of calling her Juke.

Out of Place, 2001

Em never told Tee. Didn't have the chance. First the stripe on the do-it-yourself home pregnancy test. Elation. *Joy grows inside me.* Then disbelief, hesitation. Terror. Dismay. She was well over 40! Halfway to 50. They'd just been through the Dover business and were spending some weeks apart, incommunicado, by unspoken agreement, it seemed. Their last time together, at his apartment, had been raw, excruciating for them both. No phone calls since, no notes or dried leaves or nipped flowers slipped into Messenger Mail or under the wiper blade of her parked car. Not one email. Tee was hurt, clearly, and was, perhaps, punishing her. Waiting her out.

The award: she should have been indignant; how dare he be angry and sullen about something so positive and affirming for her? Truth be told, Em felt horrible about her knee-jerk impulse to flee, about not being more patient about his reaction to her news. But she had also been relieved. The separation from Tee would be temporary, she believed that, of course, but it would give her space, for a few days, a week or two, to think about the Dover and what it might mean for her and for her daughter, especially given Paul's "dalliances," sexual and otherwise, which seemed to preoccupy him more and more of late.

But a pregnancy! That was something else altogether. It was impossible. Within the week after the apartment

parting: fatigue, tender breasts, nausea she'd chalked up to nerves had finally sent her to the drug store and into the family bathroom with an at-home pregnancy test. And there was, suddenly, this other "positive" news—this blue, unlikely, unlooked-for stripe, undeniable in the dark morning shadowing the sink, the tub. How far along was she, she wondered? At her age, her periods had become erratic; she hadn't worried much about being late.

There was her daughter to consider in all of this, first and foremost, who was now a very precocious fifteen. Also Paul, despite his remoteness and his own affairs. The fact that they rarely had sex was a worry, too. Would this expose Tee, her own betrayal? And then there was her work! And Tee himself. Was there room in his life, his headspace, for a child? How to fit a baby into this double, secret life and a half they'd made for themselves? She scoffed. The test must be wrong. She was too old to conceive! It was no doubt a false positive, a mistake. A fluke of "the change," as some called it. Sit on it, she told herself. Wait a bit. Wait and see.

So she kept working, hard, pushing herself, pushing Tee to the back of her mind every time he surfaced, which was often. It was nearly the end of the spring term, lots of critiques to schedule, student shows to put up. Surely he was busy now, too. To outpace her qualms, she started spending nights in the studio. She threw her shoulder out lifting a stack of lithography stones. Her whole body ached.

Then the spotting. Period at last, she thought, there in the print shop unisex bathroom, filled with relief. But also a fleeting twinge of source-less sadness.

Two days later, she collapsed in the print shop during a student critique. Most students were not even aware she was

married, she wore no rings—what the chemicals did to gems and metals—but they knew to call an ambulance for help.

Paul received a message at his office in DC from the hospital in Virginia. Suddenly all of the complex deflections and delays, the stallings, diversions, and surfaces of his own life with Em gained dimension, crystallized into something about her he could actually control. Long detached from his wife and daughter, the emergency sharpened into what, he would tell himself, had all of this time been a kind of love.

After two weeks in the ICU following a ruptured ectopic pregnancy, Em was deemed able to be moved. "Out of place," Em learned, was what "ectopic" meant. Before a week was out, Paul, officious, tense, and hypocritically attentive, had driven Em and their daughter north to an apartment, a New England seaside town they'd sometimes visited on vacation in years past. Too weary and emotional at the time to object, unreachable by anyone thanks to Paul's strenuous oversight and unspoken but nonetheless manifestly self-righteous anger (this pregnancy, this "baby," after all, could not have been his, given the fact that he'd secretly had a vasectomy years ago, just not cut out for fatherhood, he'd told himself), Em tried to settle herself, grateful to be alive, newly aware of and thankful for her living daughter's presence, attention, and need of her. Be mother first, she'd told herself. Recover.

Em was too tired and constrained, in those first summer months in the little town beside the sea, to make any sort of first move toward reunion with Tee, who had already withdrawn from her, it seemed, and so she let the machinery of the world, the commitments that her younger self had charted years ago, reclaim her. She relinquished her teaching

job in Virginia, at first just temporarily, and threw herself into fulfilling her Dover genius term.

She worked from rooms in a refurbished fishery, embodying a series she'd sketched out over the past couple of years called "The Incarnation Series." She'd somehow lost her notes for the series, but she worked from memory. She bought an old Vandercook Press with her prize money, funds which she also used to assemble a bare bones studio from what was already there—plumbing, sinks, tables, ventilation. She called her studio "The Fishhouse," after the Elizabeth Bishop poem. The incarnation/refrigerator project took on new resonance for her, exiled as she was, like Virgil beside the sea. She had to reimagine the whole endeavor from scratch. Doing site visits at various lobster shacks, factories, canning plants, up-scale restaurants, she took candid, "surprise visit" photographs of deep freezers, meat lockers, home refrigerators, turning them into prints at once eerily arctic and visceral, especially timely in an era of glacial melting and plastic-clogged, endangered waterways and oceans. Near the end of her fellowship, Em had a small show of her ice-box incarnation prints at a gallery in New York. She'd collaborated on the series with a dancer friend, who had performed at the opening, nude from waist to neck, which caused a little stir, and someone was talking about doing a short documentary about the work and the show.

She also became a better, more attentive mother to her daughter, who was evolving from the oblivious ease of her late girlhood into a scarily savvy teenager. Meanwhile, Paul, crisis with Em averted, returned before long to his philandering ways. Emotional affairs, mostly. His paralyzing fear of Em's own emotional and, at least for the moment, relative

financial independence, his daughter's new agency and, he thought, irking lack of respect for him, and his wife's crazy talent drove him, finally and seriously, into the arms of a slightly younger woman, an architect, a lovely person, Iranian, much better than he deserved as he was the first to admit, a consultant with his agency. They adopted twin Chinese girls and were raising them on two continents. These were changes for which he compensated Em with a relatively amicable divorce and a small settlement that, along with the remains of her banked Dover prizemoney, was substantial enough to allow her, finally, to believe in a life in which, if she worked hard, she might feel secure, in which she might take risks she never dreamed might be hers to take, beyond the tremendous risk she'd taken to be with Tee. A risk that struck her even now as inextricably linked to everything she was and would be for the rest of her life.

She started a lino-cut workshop for local teenage girls at The Fishhouse on Thursday evenings, with her daughter signing on as her first assistant. She partnered with a few local middle and high schools, and conducted a kind of open house, with the school-tapped girls and some of their friends dropping in. At first it was just five girls from two different junior high schools. At its height, twenty or more adolescent women would make their way to the ramshackle docks, each Thursday evenings at about 7 PM.

Em provided the materials, again with her prize money—stacks of lino plates she cut herself from squares of linoleum flooring she bought at a local hardware store, cutters, ink, rollers, paper—very low-end and approachable printmaking—as well as plates of brownies, jugs of cider. Local girls, many of them troubled by issues at home, chosen by their

teachers and counselors, came to the studio to carve plates, girls whose bodies were often heavily inked with intricate tattoos and piercings, and who sometimes cut their own bodies or pulled out their own hair—eyebrows, lashes, head—and most of whom had never even thought about making art, let alone a print.

Many were reserved at first, but Em showed them how it wasn't necessary to even draw well to make a print. A hot iron against a cloth (or against a child's face, one of the girls pointed out) could be a print. What does it mean, she asked them, to mark, to be marked? In the studio, the girls inked their mouths, thumbs, elbows, buttocks, printed newspaper, curtains, dishcloths, men's underwear, each other's bodies. "Eternity," said Em, "is in love with the productions of time.'" That's William Blake, she said, "a revolutionary," and showed them the colored plates of his *Songs*, the images—transgressive—in his *Notebook*. One of the girls began calling herself "Nobodaddy" after a word they'd seen in Blake's jottings. Imagine that great mind dulled on Prozac, Em had said.

Drawing from her stacks of big, glossy books, she showed them the city street prints of Helen Frank. The grids of Agnes Martin. In turn they played for her their favorite music, groups like Destiny's Child, Animal Collective, Blaque. Salt-N-Pepa. 4 on the Floor. They made Em dance with them to "Bootilicious" and "R U Ready." Together they pored over Satrapi's *Persepolis* and a rogue copy of Tokyopop's *Manga*. They held annual shows of their workshop productions, first at the studio and then, when they needed more space, at a local community center. They got a small write-up about the project in *The Globe*. Riffing on the word "matrix," term for the surface from which a print is pulled, they called themselves the

"Matrichix." They printed fabrics, sold curtains, bedspreads, t-shirts, messenger bags, camisoles, thongs. One of her former pupils was now at RISD. Another had founded and was running an organization offering fellowships for women artists who had to work time-consuming administrative arts-related jobs in the city. Yet another had her own celebrity tattoo shop, known well beyond the Boston area.

But as the heavy lifting and toxic chemicals of printmaking began to take a toll on Em physically, her lungs, her hands, her energy, she herself took another risk and enrolled in graduate courses at a nearby university, where, by far the oldest in her cohort, she finished up surprisingly quickly a PhD in Victorian literature that she'd started years ago while she was teaching printmaking in Virginia, eventually securing a part-time teaching job in literature at a small, nearby college.

After the divorce, Emma never considered re-marrying. True, she did try more than a couple times not so much to contact Tee, but to learn what he was up to (how, she'd wondered, did a person in this day and age, not Have an Internet Presence At All?). No website, nothing on Amazon but that one poetry book, *Our Hour*, now out of print (not even Em's artwork on the author page, "No Image Available," she read). No one from the university where they'd both worked nearly two decades ago bothered to answer her queries at all. Did anyone read or answer email anymore? she wondered. She herself mostly stayed off of what she called "Social Medea." No one offered a sense of where he'd landed, so in-the-dark-of-night had been his sudden exodus from his former life. No obituary, either. Thank goodness for that, she thought, if that meant he were still alive and happy somewhere.

Finally, Em had to put her curiosity aside and tried to honor Tee's loner ways as, she had to admit, despite her full life, she tried to honor her own. She elected to believe, rightly or wrongly, that her need for a separate creative life, and of a private existence with her daughter, would have always been a source of unsolvable pain for him, for them both. That was why he'd disappeared, wasn't it? That's why I did, too, she decided. As for their lovemaking, which had been breathtaking, she found herself grateful for it every day.

He sees me, she'd say to herself, putting on her clothes in the morning, taking them off at night, touching herself. In bed, knees apart, making the letter "m," or bent upright, tenting the sheet, her mouth became his mouth, breasts wet with transport of saliva making nipples startle, as beneath his tongue, the night air coming in the open window cooling them, and her hands his hands, too, and vice versa, V of the pointer and tall fingers, a slight pinch here, then here, then a flat palm passing from breast to breast calming, then arousing, saying wait, wait, no need to rush, it's going to happen, Emma, Em, Em, go slow, turn on your side, does this hurt, am I hurting you, make time wait for you, for us, as V of the pointer and tall fingers now score the inner thigh, the right, the left, then back to breasts, palming, pinching, it hurts good, she says, it does he says, smell of his breath at the fork of her, wait, wait, I'm right here, you're safe, speaking in tongues as another mouth-whetted finger reaches behind to wiggle up the anus, bright burst of nerve endings, primal how all the orifices feel as one, his, hers, theirs, mine, so that, inside themself herself himself at last, fingers meet cock meet fingers through walls of velvet flesh, sometimes flipping over onto stomach this way, bedclothes binding ankles, rising up

on knees, then rolling back onto the spine's ladder, slipping among linens from mattress to floor, whole body deranging at last as if being reborn into ceiling, the sky beyond, its furniture of stars and planets and mythic milky way, heaven dipping down toward us, lapping the ocean inside me, you, Tee, Em, tidal, coming, coming, holding, rocking us both as close as souls who once knew each other in bodies can possibly be.

And in this way, as the many weeks became months and then years, Em was not alone but reminded of all the ways Tee had shaped and loved her body, and helped her to love it too, love it even, or especially, as it aged, inexorably, right along with her.

Capertons, 2017

Of course he'd found out about Em, that long-ago spring in the weeks he was nursing his hurt about her Dover. Universities, especially in small towns, are petri dishes. Fish bowls. Em's collapse at school, her ectopic pregnancy, hospitalization, the outcome, her enforced exile (he could just imagine Gray Top engineering the whole thing)—he'd heard it all from colleagues who had heard about it from Em's students, who'd in turn heard it from their other teachers, in strictest confidence. Of course he wondered if the lost child had been his. He thought it probably was, though he had no real idea about Paul and what went on there. And while he and Em were usually careful, they sometimes were not, either too rapt and urgent in their captured moments—on the studio pallet, the floor of his office—or trusting themselves, perhaps mistakenly as it turned out, to be too old to worry about things like fertility, like birth control, things like condoms, which, frankly, neither one of them much cared to use.

He waited for her to call him, to write to him. He had, after all, a right to know the truth from her. He wanted to be summoned and told. On some level, too, he wanted to apologize. And be forgiven.

No letter came. No email. And then, unlooked-for, arrived the news, by registered post (how his heart had leapt at first, believing the envelope to have come from Em), of his aunt's death and his sudden inheritance of The Hole, a bequest

that offered up to Tee a reprieve, the chance to bow out, to begin again.

He'd taken the out. And it had been, after all, a good life for him, the massive house, the seclusion, the clocks, the tinkering, interactions he could control, the insomnia, the long mountain walks.

But now that Juke had intruded—that wasn't right, now that she had *arrived* in his solitary life, as bluntly and unexpectedly as Em had once, long ago, upended his world by entering and then leaving it—it was impossible not to confront his long hurt and loneliness, hard not to see this silver-haired miracle ("what is a miracle, if not the intrusion of one world into another?" he'd read somewhere, where? Pynchon?), sitting quietly beside him, using needle-nose pliers to twist the strange odd charms of abandoned timepieces into earrings, necklaces, hard not to feel her presence as some reclamation of Em and their lost child—that story—which was Love—love that they had so recklessly, essentially, and hungrily made, and then appeared to lose forever.

One morning in January, about a month after Juke had materialized, he drove off before she had awakened, making his way to Capertons with the sole intention, at last, of asking for clues, evidence, explanation.

He'd put this off, time and time again over the past weeks. Meantime, he and Juke washed the kimono, which she continued to wear each night, sleeping in his old bed while he slept on the futon. They gathered up from the attic and burned her one torn and mud-caked shoe (they never found the other) and clothes in an oil can in the yard, and had taken a trip all the way to West Virginia to buy for her, at a Target, jeans, a sweater, underwear. A warm coat. Socks. Boots.

But as each day passed, as Tee and Juke moved through the workshop, the kitchen, the yard, not touching, the space between them grew more charged.

Before anything happened, before she brushed his arm, before he would ask her if he might hold her, he felt he must try to learn what he could about her. If there was anything for him to learn in this mystery. For her sake, too. For anyone who might have lost her. He admitted that for him to lose her now would be almost unbearable. His heart pounded as he stepped into Capertons, door bells jangling.

To his great relief, no one at the store had heard of anyone gone missing. The men around the stove consulted each other, all shook their heads, checking and re-checking their phones. Nura, wrapped in a fringed wool shawl, came in while they were musing, stamping snow off her boots. She would know, if anyone would, Tee thought, her reach into the woods and wider world, into situations domestic and transgressive, being much broader than that of most of the men. She gazed at Tee searchingly for a moment after he asked, but shook her head and had to agree with the men that no, she'd heard nothing about an abused spouse or any sort of imperiled or lost person. No regional accident of car or prop plane, no escape from the prison or hospital reported in the last six months, the men's Google searches also confirmed. No lost hiker or runaway. Nothing.

"Why you asking," Debussy queried, loading up Tee's box. He looked at Tee. "You smiling, Trey? That a smile?" Tee shook his head. He supposed he would have to bring Juke by to meet them all, one of these days.

On the drive back to The Hole, fields and orchards spread out on either side of the road, monochromatic and

Breughelian, broad swaths of white snow stitched with dark hedgerows, crows, the creeks black and fresh and running, Tee thought of Juke, and of how when he'd asked her if that name, Juke, might suit her, she'd wept into her hands. He had not seen her cry until that moment. His heart had dropped. He thought of Em, her impulse to escape. He couldn't help it. He'd made a mistake, overstepped.

Juke's lifted face was her answer. "O, Tee," she said. "Juke. Juke. Why, yes. Juke. Please, please call me Juke."

Is this what it meant, then, not just to acknowledge but to accept, to believe in a gift, he wondered, hands at the wheel, Monteverdi on the CD player as he began his drive back to The Hole? To trust in the force of a seam blown open in the fabric of the universe, through which love might slip in as well as out? As Em had once entered his life, long ago, making all things possible. Juke was not Em. But was Juke . . . real? Was she seasonal, like the chimney swifts, migratory, driven by unseen forces that would propel her away from him as magnetically as she'd arrived? Was she criminal? Redeemed? An amnesiac? Delusional? A figment? Forgiveness? Grace itself?

His long-held anxiety, guilt, fear, and anger at Em, and at himself, reawakened by these questions about Juke, all of this jolted inside him, bird in a cage, bat in a house, welled up tightly, battering, burning his chest. He belched, and fire shot through him. He felt the pressure physically, heavily, erupting at his clavicles, his throat, behind his eyes. His hands went numb. Was this it, then? Was he about to die? A shame, a shame, he thought, strangely calm, for this to happen just as his metaphorical heart was reassembling.

Tee pulled off the narrow road, pressed his foot hard on the brake. He held onto his last breath for as long as he

could, hands frozen on the wheel, while the engine ran and Monteverdi's counterpoint filled the car. Centuries of cloud passed across the windshield. Leaves, birds. Grace notes. Mordents. *We spend our years as a tale that is told.* That came to him from childhood, a psalm. He saw the phrase write itself in the air and disappear. Ears pounding, eyes tearing up, vessels surging, skull about to burst, Tee held, held, and then, when he could no longer stop it, expelled with a groan of death or birth nearly two decades of fraught and freighted air.

He sat afterwards for a long while. When he came to, his foot was still on the brake, the engine running, the steering wheel was in his fists. He unclenched, wiggled his fingers. Wind rocked the small car. A white, berry-flecked spill of bird shit splatted against the windshield. Monteverdi's singers sang their madrigals. Still here, he thought. He took another, cleansing, sparkling, trusting breath. Then headed home.

PART THREE

Paradise

New York City, January 2017

Maddie's hand lit up and buzzed. She and her mother had just come down from a stroll on the High Line, which had been fine and brisk and golden in the late January afternoon, gilt clouds in armada formations, the usual mix of tourists, skater-boys and girls, nannies pushing elaborate strollers, walkers in puffer coats, readers hunched with their books on benches, loners. Birds flitting low among the shrubberies. Some Christmas lights still lit in apartment windows they could see into, and taped-up "Not My President" signs. Now they were heading for a drink before they made their way to Tribeca for a late dinner with this Asa that Marlise had been hearing so much about, the book designer. Then Maddie and Asa would take the train back to Brooklyn, and Marlise would return to her hotel, where she needed to think a bit more about the talk she was presenting tomorrow to some graduate students at the New School. It wasn't a big visit; just guest-teaching a seminar for a professor, a younger woman who had been her classmate in graduate school. "Juvenilia, or The Glass Self," Marlise was calling it, though large parts of her argument weren't quite worked through. She hoped to engage the students in a conversation about the Brontë children's imaginary worlds, Glass Town, in particular, and about some ideas she'd been tossing around about childhood as a glass-like construction (what did Shakespeare call the self, a "glassy essence"?), an asylum, in both connotations of the word—imprisonment

and freedom—and to delve into some of Deleuze's notions of the fold, about hidden and manifest identities, with a focus on the "apprentice pieces" of Emily Brontë and Robert Hayden.

Blah, blah. She knew this would all sound very old-fashioned to the students. It was still weird for her, this life as a sort of literary scholar, the unexpected attention she received in the wake of a small book she'd published on the marginalia of a number of Victorian women diarists. Could she make that work, she wondered, the baroque secrecy and the transparent paradox of glass? Actually, she was thinking hard about a glassy martini in a nice dark bar.

They continued walking, arm in arm, as Maddie chatted on her phone with one of her buyers. It was chillier on the street than it had been up on the sun-struck High Line. Marlise recalled the first time, five years ago or more, maybe, that she'd watched in wonder as her daughter looked down into the phone in her palm, unearthing with her fingertips the birthdate of Cindy Sherman, whose show they'd just seen at the MoMA, while at the same time cancelling a dinner reservation at one place and booking another, calculating, too, how long it would take them to get there if they walked or if they took a taxi or the train, and Maddie, responding to a text and sending another, never missing a step, keeping one hand at Marlise's elbow, steering her down the Avenue without, Marlise knew, wanting to appear to be doing so, keeping them going in the right direction. It was always Marlise's inclination, though she herself now possessed such a phone and could in fact feel it buzzing at her hip in her cross-body bag, to stop when she was lost, move out of the crush of sidewalk bodies, and rummage for a paper map. Glancing around now, it seemed to Marlise that

everyone was looking down into lambent, upturned palms. Prophets. Saints, all of them.

As Maddie talked on the phone, Marlise thought about the show of Emily Dickinson ephemera they'd seen that afternoon at the grand old Pierpont Morgan Library. Or simply the Morgan, as they called it now. Years ago, Marlise had witnessed there a pair of Charlotte Brontë's tiny folded gloves in a case, no wider than a gull's feather. Anyway, the Dickinson show had been small, but thrilling for Marlise—that lock of red hair (Marlise had seen that before, in a library at Amherst), the hallucinatory wallpaper, restored and displayed. No wonder Dickinson woke in the wee hours, unable to sleep through the birdsong amidst all the blinding pink florals.

Not surprisingly, Maddie had been taken with the Herbarium that Dickinson had assembled when she was a girl, and began making some sketches from the pages on view, in her notebook. Maddie's own drawings and designs, recently incorporating her studies of Islamic calligraphy she'd first seen on a visit to her father and his new wife at Somerset House in London, were now being shown in a few places, including galleries abroad, in addition to being turned into couture fabrics for dresses, coats, upholstery. She was working on a couple of collaborative art books, as well, including one for children. Marlise was wearing one of Maddie's creations now, a tawny heavy sweater coat embroidered at the sleeves and hem with intricate, whimsical silk concoctions: stickleburrs, winged seeds, leaf tatter, as though she'd just come in from a traipse in the fields.

Marlise gazed a while at Dickinson's Bible, tome plundered by that wild, iconoclastic mind for clues to what immensities and mysteries lay beyond this mortal coil. Maddie, continuing

to scribble onto her pages ideas from the Herbarium, had said, as though she had eyes in the back of her head, "Why encase it in glass? Why not let us see inside it?" Yes, Marlise could see the point to that. Why not? She also thought she might know why not.

She crossed the room and stood looking over Maddie's shoulder. "To me," she said, "these herbarium pages have always felt like Dickinson's poems."

"Like a translation of them?" Maddie asked, peering once more at the preserved foliage on display, then closing up her sketchbook and tucking it into her backpack. "Something figurative? Mimetic, visually?" Marlise gave Maddie a hug. "Maybe. More like a premonition, the perfume or essence of them. Something she'd intuited in girlhood, something that was yet to manifest in her poetry. Ready to go?"

After Maddie ended her phone call, they continued walking, arms linked. Maddie turned her luminous, beautiful face toward her mother's. "Aren't you going to ask me about Paul?"

"Okay, how is your father?"

"Doing well. Old, though. Old-ish. Bald! He could only stay one night, passing through. Samira and the kids weren't with him this time, the banned countries, you know. After all the time she worked in the states. He had to get back overseas. The twins are in something like middle school now, can you believe it?"

She gave Maddie a smile. Marlise was glad that Maddie seemed comfortable at last with the divorce and Paul's remarriage, his move, his new job, new family. It had been years ago, and very hard then. But not hard any longer, she hoped.

"I'm hungry," Marlise said. "Where is dinner?"

A place recommended by a chef friend of Asa's, but there

were no early reservations available, Maddie was saying, distracted suddenly as they turned a corner onto a side street navy blue with building shadow, though the cornices, rooftops, and water towers still blazed with winter sun. "We'll get our drink at the Red Cat, it's just up ahead, but first let's duck in here. I've been wanting to see this."

These Chelsea galleries, thought Marlise. Big blank brick walls and you'd think nothing here, old warehouses, an industrial door or two, often no signage, but inside, suddenly and always, opening up into something unexpected and often wonderful. The way she'd slipped into a Basquiat show by accident a couple of years ago, and found herself inside a wonderland of rooms hung with paintings and drawings of his she'd never seen before or since. She sometimes wondered if she'd dreamed the whole thing.

Maddie knew Elle, the young woman at the desk, and Marlise, after introducing herself, wandered into the gallery space while behind her Maddie lingered to talk with her friend.

Marlise took one step more, then stopped. She had an eerie feeling in her scalp and limbs, the way she sometimes felt before a migraine descended or if she were lowering a window against an electrical storm. The room was dim, with only the white walls spot-lit, hung with paintings. There was a door opening into a room beyond. Behind her, Elle was saying "yes, a retrospective. Works by the owner's brother.... you know, Raina Newman, her main gallery is the famous one, in Geneva... the artist died decades ago, barely into his twenties." And "Oh," she said, louder now, so Maddie's mother could hear, "the show proceeds chronologically, earliest work to the stuff he was doing just before he died. Just go on through at your own pace."

And here they were, the paintings Marlise had seen so long ago on a postcard shown to her by someone, one of the aides, at the Institute. The ones that had been given an early showing in Philadelphia back when Silas was just a patient in his teens. They were much larger than she'd imagined them to be. The letters on the wall said "The Choke-Her Series (1965–1968)," along with excerpts from some contemporary reviews and some new commentary.

Maddie and Elle had joined Marlise, who was finding it hard to catch her breath. "Apparently they're of the mother," Elle was explaining. "A complicated relationship, I'd say."

"Ha, ha, I'd never want to choke YOU, Ma," said Maddie. Marlise squeezed Maddie's hand. "These early pieces are prescient," Elle continued, "especially considering that the artist kills himself in his mother's apartment when he's only twenty-one. An overdose, apparently. An old stash of drugs he'd had hidden away. The very drugs they gave him when he was hospitalized, to cure him, if you can believe that."

As the young women moved into the next room, Elle was saying, "the family thinks he was depressed because, after running away from a hospital in a fugue state of some sort and being readmitted and given a series of ECT shocks, he'd been turned down for an NEA grant. The blow of that rejection apparently crushed him. But who hasn't been overlooked for one of those, I've been turned down every year I've applied, haven't you? And I'm over 30!"

Marlise felt as if she might faint. Through a blur of tears she looked down at the flyer Maddie had pressed into her hand. "Disenfranchised Bodies: A Retrospective of the Precocious Paintings of Silas Newman."

What had happened to Silas?

Not Paul, not Tee, not even Maddie, no one living in her world knew about those years in Marlise's life. About how Marlise had so long ago, in another story, been orphaned, sent to school, hospitalized for not eating until her trust fund ran out. How she had stayed for a while, unsupervised, and then fallen unconscious in an old family farmhouse during a blizzard when she was almost fifteen. None of them knew about the strange circumstances that led her Uncle Cole, dying of terminal cancer, to find her there, where he'd gone to kill himself, or about the strange man, a criminal as it turned out, who drove them through thigh-high drifts of belting snow and wind in the blazing cab of a pick-up truck to an emergency room. Nor did they know of her subsequent adoption by her god-father Maurice Miles, how she'd changed her last name to his and started going for a long time by Emma, Em, a subconscious effort, maybe, to start anew, and also to separate her real name from Silas's (what had he said? "Look, your name contains mine!"), though she started going by Marlise again, Marlise Miles, years later, once her divorce from Paul was final. None of them knew about her life before art school, marriage, motherhood. No one but Tee himself knew she'd fallen in mid-life into life-changing extra-marital love with a man from whom she'd been long separated, but who had helped her turn, at last, through ardor and resistance, to an embodied life and a desire to endure.

Standing before the paintings she'd seen printed on a postcard so long ago, Marlise allowed a memory to seep back from the time after she'd been driven through the snowstorm and was reclaimed by good old Maurice, who returned to New Jersey from the West Coast to adopt her. They settled

into a split-level on a mid-state cul de sac, where Maurice, more or less abandoned by his own sons and step-children, had managed from a home office what money had come of Cole's holdings and the Paradise Close estate sale for Marlise (and himself, presumably). After some sessions with a local psychiatrist—the only one accredited in the New Brunswick area—Marlise, going by Emma, had enrolled in a large public high school, where she delved into and excelled in the study of English and studio art, life drawing at first, then print-making, and made friends with a group of drama friends who accepted her utterly, from the start, drawing her peripherally into their world of high school theater and regaling her with accounts of their weekend trips into the burgeoning queer scene in Manhattan, where their beauty and youth gave them purchase in clubs and drag shows. These gamine boys and bold girls, smoking under the shelters between buildings, talking about Ionesco, *Siddhartha*, Roxy Music—reminded her of Silas, but without his possessiveness and paranoia.

Accepted without question, but also not anyone's particular focus, she began to recover. You're sexier than you were when you showed up, her friends said. We made you sexier. She floated among them, a virgin, but that was okay, too. What excited her most those days: the outline of red maple leaves against sky. The art she was beginning to make. A line from a poem, "it is the blight man was born for. / It is Margaret you mourn for." A cold, sugary swallow of ripe pear. The fragrance of a freshly pulled linoleum print, the inks still wet and rife with root-like musk.

When it was time for college, she'd gotten into all the art schools to which she'd applied, and focused her studies in

intaglio printmaking, always serious, serious, but also, again, venturing into the safe but fluid shoals of theater through connections with a few of her friends from high school, also now attending the same fine arts college. Why, now, in this Chelsea gallery, standing before the early work of Silas Newman, was she thinking not about her own former life as an artist, her early success in showing her work, in landing a university job teaching printmaking, even earning a big award for her projects, her later work in the Fishhouse studio with adolescent girls, but rather of that one cast party after a student-directed production of *The Tempest* in the late winter of her senior undergraduate year? The director had decided to cast five women to play the part of Ariel, that most exquisite shape-shifter, appearing first here, then there, orchestrating, deploying, disappearing into air. Marlise was pressed into service as one of them. We're the pussy posse, said Axel, another Ariel, a girl from Marlise's poli-sci class who wore men's dress shirts and ties and who gave Marlise long, frank admiring looks during boring afternoon discussions of the new Carter presidency and the recent election. It had been liberating and, she had to admit, fun to be out of the print studio and part of a sweaty throng of fluid, androgynous Shakespearean spirits, dressing and undressing in a crowded space backstage, acting as one manifold and antic whole.

Her own Ariel-time on stage was brief, her speech from Act II addressing Prospero's old advisor, Gonzalo:

> My master through his art foresees the danger
> That you, his friend, are in, and sends me forth
> (For else his project dies) to keep them living.

After delivering her handful of lines, she had to sing ("I can't sing," she'd protested. "The lady," Axel had said, "doth protest too much, methinks"), and so sing she did, as well as she could, into the shapely ear of Eugene, a rather twiggy Gonzalo, a boy she'd known since high school and who would, Marlise later learn, die of the AIDS so many of her former high school friends had unwittingly contracted back in those freewheeling, carefree days. "While you do snoring lie," she croaked out as best she could,

> Open-eyed conspiracy
> His time doth take.
> If of life you keep a care,
> Shake off a slumber and beware.
> Awake, awake!

The cast party after the last performance had been at the off-campus house of a group of graduate student thespians. Amidst the drinking, the skunky sea-drift of pot, there had been dancing and impromptu recitations—the usual de rigeur and raucous throw-down competitions of Shakespearean profanity, delivered from tabletops and sofas—"Thou whoreson zed, thou unnecessary letter!" and "Thy wit's as thick as Tewkesbury mustard"—theater people were so refreshingly self-conscious—but other lines as well, things Marlise didn't recognize—"Try again. Fail again. Fail better"—and some she did. Axel, who, Marlise realized, reminded her of that long-ago girl with the beaver coat, grabbed Marlise's hands mid-rave, dropped to her knees, singing "for thou art / As glorious as to this night, being o'er my head, / As is a winged messenger of heaven / Unto the white-upturned wondering eyes

/of mortals," before leaping to her feet and kissing Marlise deeply on the mouth.

With the unexpected sensation of wine and smoke from Axel's tongue inside her, Marlise, Emma, felt the many stories of her body begin to stir. She didn't pull away after the kiss, and Axel stood there, grinning. And then, as if by stage direction or Prosperian orchestration, an odd early March thunderstorm that had been rumbling around the outskirts of town all evening and brewing into the wee hours finally crashed over the house, and the lights dimmed, crackled. On. Off. On again. And went dark.

Complete silence followed, also as if by magical command. The record on the stereo skidded statically to a halt in the pong of sweat, cannabis, yeasty beer, spilled wine. Somewhere a clock ticked. Shadowy sensations of other bodies. Bodies slowly moving. A hand brushed her breast. Lips touched lips, smoke and wine of Axel again in her mouth. A hand slipped down between her belly and blue jean zipper, another up her shirt. Her nipples stiffened. She felt fingers up inside her. Wet there. Marlise reaching out, too, now, but where, to whom? On her knees. Someone, Axel?, unzipping, then a surprise, an erect cock, velvet skin, warm against her face. In her mouth. The valentine tip of it. Now in her hand. Someone tugging at her jeans. She slipped out of them with one hand, the other still holding the warm swelling cock. Bigger now. And coming in a hot silky jet just as she slipped it between her legs. Smell of ocean. What had Silas asked her, long ago, in the sunroom of the Institute? Can you smell the seawater in the air? She could. She did. More tumble then, sweating bodies inside each other, turning into each other everywhere. Rapid breathing, gasps,

grunts, growlings in the dark. Sighs. Small cries. Panting. No words.

By daybreak, the storm had blown off, but there was still no electricity in the house. Enthralled at the heaps of partly clothed, sleeping bodies around her in the pearly dawn, Marlise dressed, gathered up her things and walked back to her dorm. A garbage truck groaned past, rank with vegetable peelings, vinegar, and wet newspaper. First birds in the sycamores. Whiff of green sap and storm-drenched mulch. A glimmer of almost spring. Of being in her body. "Awake!" she sang aloud. "Awake!"

For weeks afterward, as crocuses, snowdrops, winter-blooming jasmine emerged along the walkways of the quad, the partygoers flashed bruises, exchanged secret smiles in hallways, across classrooms and studios. Then one of the Ariels, Maxine, learned she was pregnant and had to go into the city for an abortion. The high of that night of the cast party began to wane. And then, suddenly, in late March, Maurice died of complications of undiagnosed lung cancer. A sadly underwhelming funeral was held for him back at the New Jersey split-level, organized by the long-ago divorced and suddenly italicized Sylvie, who flew over from England to organize things. Clusters of unreconciled step-children crowded the small rooms, drunk and milling about in suits. Em was worried—missed classes and studio time (Em had her senior show to get ready!)—all postponed temporarily by a series of meetings with lawyers.

Finally back at school, leaving the studio at dawn after a full night of work during the last week of classes, Marlise had been stopped by Paul, who was at that time a junior professor in the JAG fiscal law program and who was heading down to

DC in the fall for a new job in the public sector. He asked her if she might like to have a coffee with him. He'd seen her in *The Tempest*, he said. Really, Marlise had wondered. And he'd seen her senior show, also, he said, which had opened at the student gallery space the week before. He thought she was very good. He had some gallery contacts. Would she be interested?

'You stalking me?' Marlise had asked. She kept walking. He kept pace. One thing led to the next, and within months, Marlise, as Emma Miles, moved to Virginia with Paul, who worked for the government in the District, but who also held a part-time professorship at a Virginia university. When they married, she kept her new name, Emma Miles. Paul was able to arrange an adjunct job for her in the studio art department on the merits of her art school degree and her luminous work, which she was beginning to show and sell. That part-time job would turn into a professorship of her own. Meanwhile, she also began to take graduate courses in English, the study of Victorian literature long a road not taken for her. Gazing now at Silas's choke-hold paintings all these years later, Marlise acknowledged that, with Maurice dead, graduation looming, legal entanglements, and so much uncertainty in her future, Paul had offered her stability, money, marital sex, a way out of the thrilling but confusing spell into which the beginnings of her artistic and sexual awakening had thrown her, an awakening that had probably begun long ago, with Silas, his mouth circling her ears, kissing her inner thigh, showing her his paintings, and that was later fulfilled so wildly and unexpectedly by Tee in the short but life-altering time they'd had together.

After several attempts, she'd decided not to try to track down Tee, believing that he would have wanted it that

way, finally, especially since she'd not heard from him and because she'd failed to reach him. Her monk. Besides, she felt him with her, all the time—his voice in her ear, slow down, make time, Emma, Em. But she'd never stopped trying to find Silas, and in many ways they, Tee and Silas, were, to her, inextricably linked. Both were still inside her, but Tee's presence was still so physical, no doubt because of their sexual bond. Her relationship with Silas had been inchoate, and so he kept eluding her, despite the fact that he'd been the first person to really see and try to truly know her. She learned that Silas had run away from the Institute and evaporated into the very same blizzard through which Marlise herself had been rushed back to life. The hospital was unable legally to release his medical and psychiatric records to her, or any family contact information. Judging by the dates on the exhibition paper she now held onto, as if for dear life, he'd lived just a year after that. What had happened in that time? Where had he gone? How had he landed back in Switzerland with his parents who'd seemed to want him electro-convulsed and put away? What had driven him, at last, to end his life?

As recently as a year ago, Marlise had typed his name again into Google, but little came up, just the same two, old archived newspaper notices from the 70s. Not even a mention on a "bad dad" site, notice of a petty crime, or reminder of a neighborhood association lawn-mowing assignment, let alone an image of a person, a painting. No Linked-In profile, no Facebook account. Not even another Silas Newman. No obituary. She, Marlise, was sixty-one. If Silas were alive, he'd be pushing seventy. Perhaps he'd become a spy. She'd entertained that thought. Gone off the grid, putting all of that bi-polar paranoia to government use. Certainly there were

many reasons to be afraid, especially these days. Standing in the dark gallery, she could guess now that the way he had died, by suicide, and the times being what they were then, no Internet, and his living with distant, estranged family abroad—well, somehow it had all been suppressed. And now, the exhibition brochure in her hands told her, the paintings that Silas's sister, the gallery owner, had quietly been locating and acquiring over the years since his death, were being brought together and shown for the first time in a series of shows, first on the continent and now in the states.

Otto's Cabin, 1971

As a blizzard buffeted the small house on the abandoned wine slopes of Paradise Close and Marlise lay in peril in an upper story of a big house not far away, Silas slept heavily in Otto's cot for two days without waking, during which time Otto, who nodded off in the chair by the bed or on the floor beside the bed, slept, too, but stirred often to check on him, adjusting his blankets, palming his forehead, soaking lentils, listening to the storm, the radio, chopping carrots into orange coins, preparing a pot of soup for when the boy woke.

Otto had kept on eye on the snow that gusted the window panes and shook the cabin. As soon as he could get out, he would. He had his shovel at the ready. He would find out who this boy was. This eased the heaviness in his own chest. He would rise to the task, he would get out, he would help this unfortunate person be on his way. He believed there was a working telephone in one of the outbuildings up by the big house. Or he could walk to Ida's, enlist Bill, who had a truck. He'd seen the scars on the boy's wrists, his black nails. Surely someone would be looking for him. Otto would call a doctor. Or get him to the hospital.

When Silas finally did awaken, it was to a room filled with the excruciating glare of sun on snow and the tick-tick of dripping eves. A black cat leapt lightly up onto the mattress where he had slept for days in his wet clothes, sour with sweat, and gazed at him, eyes steadfast and gray.

Silas lay still, trying to fathom where he was, listening to the engine of the cat's body in the quiet room, his eyes slowly adjusting to the light. He registered the body in the chair beside the bed, arms folded across a blue apron. Asleep? Pushing himself up against the headboard, Silas stared, then realized that the old man who'd brought him in from the snowstorm, and kept vigil, made soup (Silas would find it waiting, ready, in a pot on the stove), that the man with kind gray eyes, now wide open, who had wrapped him in a warm blanket and gripped him in his strong arms until he'd quieted—Silas remembered all of that now—this man was dead.

Silas reached out and touched the man's large, clasped, and mottled hands. Pressing the cool flesh, holding the large hands between his own two palms, Silas began to make noise, to hum from his choked throat. Had someone sung to him once, this way, long ago, to calm him? To keep him safe? It was a song without words, a descant of rust and feathers, boughs in wind, a basket in the bulrushes, arms reaching out to pull the drifting, helpless, abandoned one to shore.

After a while, Silas remembered. He recalled himself: where he might be, and why. Marlise! Wresting himself from the covers of the bed, Silas gently closed the old man's eyes and covered his chest with a blanket. In the adjacent room, he found his own pea coat drying on a chair-back by the still warm wood stove, his boots beneath it. He pulled these on. In a covered tin can he found cat food and dropped a cupful of it into a bowl on the floor, then filled another dish with water from the stovetop kettle and set it down. Spinning around once to take in the strange beauty of the room, hung with parasols, the table piled with bolts of cloth, jars, large shears, the pot of soup, the silent cuckoo clock, Silas grabbed

his small damp bag and the shovel leaning by the door and pushed his way out into the sharp, bright world.

Down the sun-stunned, glittery slope of snow he ploughed and skidded, heart galloping, drawn magnetically through the terraced vineyard, an expansive glare, pickets poking through, and on into the shivery thicket of trees, following the river to where the woods finally cleared and before him lay the outbuildings and the large brick house of the Close itself, where surely, he prayed, Marlise was safe and sheltered. He would find her. Reunite with her at last. He began to run.

Hard to understand what he found instead, the smashed window of the side door, still ajar, a cascade of broken glass and snow across the floor, weird snow-light, the cold, empty rooms he raced through, the flights of stairs he took two at a time, calling, calling for her, breath pluming, her name ringing in the frozen air. The crimson paper lampshade on the dormer windowsill. The little cot under the dormers, Marlise's opened suitcase beside it on the floor.

What had happened to her? Who had broken into this house? Why? Where was Marlise? Had someone taken her. He must find her. He must find her and rescue her and tell her about the old man who saved him and they would do something about him. In the well of the empty suitcase lay her copy of *Jane Eyre*. He slipped it into his duffel. She would want that. Beneath the book was a stack of his letters. So they had reached her. He paused, then left them where they lay. There too was Dr. Lance's card, printed with his phone numbers, at home and at The Institute. Silas took it. As much as he didn't want to, he knew that calling The Institute was what he must do now, even if it meant his being found and returned inside. Lancelot could help him find Marlise. He

would know what to do. Silas turned the card over and saw, in pencil, "phone in shed." Shivering, shaking with terror, cold, and driven by love, Silas pivoted and ran, this time away from the house and toward the farm's cluster of outbuildings. Finally, just inside the wrenched up garage door of the packing shed: an old wall phone with a frayed cloth cord. His heart sank. But then, miraculously, a dial tone. Fingers stiff, trembling, Silas made the call.

New York City, 2017

In the next room of the gallery, Marlise stood amidst the "Meat Locker Torsos (1968–1970)," paintings that Silas had shown her once on slides, sitting beside her on the floor in the hallway at the Institute. Silas's words were there, on the wall, too, "an attempt to make visible manifestations of the soul, or lack thereof," and a critic or curator had written that they were "a prescient interpretation and indictment of their times." Here were John Mitchell and his bombs, James Lovell floating in space. There was one of Jimi Hendrix she'd not remembered seeing, a red house-cavity filled with little broken wings and crumbling, Dali-like sand-castles that reminded her of some of her own early prints. She could see now what an influence Silas had been for her in her own printmaking. And here was Tolkien, her idea if she remembered right, one big Sauronian eye taking up all the space between collarbone and waist. And the thin ribcage of Emily Brontë, a blood-soaked heath across which two star-crossed lovers held their posthumous hands.

Maddie was calling to her from the doorway to yet another room. She and Elle hadn't gotten beyond the first painting. "Come here, you have to see this."

Somehow Marlise crossed the gleaming concrete floor and stepped across the threshold of the last room of the show, the one holding Silas's late, last work, the paintings he'd done in the year before he killed himself. Standing

between Maddie and Elle, she stared into a face. "Mom, it's you! Except as, well, as a man. Okay, an *older* man than you are. But the resemblance is amazing. This person could be your father!"

It was like looking into a mirror. The same large gray eyes, the downturned mouth. Heart-shaped face. The large hands, folded into the lap of a blue smock. The sign on the wall above said, "Neglected Shades: Paintings from Paradise."

*

Elle was crouching down now beside Marlise where she leaned back against the gallery wall, legs straight out on the floor before her in black tights. "Please don't worry," Marlise said. "I just found myself feeling a little panicky for some reason. I felt I had to sit down. It's been a busy day, a full day. I'm just hungry, light-headed. I'm fine."

Now Maddie was beside her, too, patting her scalp, her shoulders, squeezing her hands, trying to make light of her mother's anxiety, but also clearly concerned. "Just do your Lamaze breathing," she was saying. "You know, like whenever you have to go to a Department meeting."

Marlise obliged. In through the nose to the count of three, out through the mouth to the count of six. "We'll get our drink," Maddie said. "We'll do that, get a cocktail, and a snack, something to eat to tide us over. Or we could go right back to the hotel. Or call a doctor? That would be fine, too. Whatever you want."

"I'm okay, I really am," said Marlise, rising without the help of the two young women, brushing down her sweater, her skirt. "It's been, I've, these are just very moving pieces. To me. It's been a very moving kind of day."

"Are you sure you're okay," Maddie said. "Because if you're sure you are, I have one more thing I have to show you before we go."

The room spun like a camera obscura as Maddie, holding Marlise's elbow, why did Maddie always feel she, Marlise, needed direction, and Marlise feared it was the frail fact that she was getting older. She didn't feel old. In fact, she suddenly felt quite young.

Maddie steered her through walls that pulsed around them, hung with window-like canvases of what looked like exotic, abstracted grids, fabrics, sewing scissors, paper lanterns, umbrellas. And then, well, it was amazing, yet there they were, gathered on one canvas, Marlise ("Look this really *is* you, just as you are *now*—the long white hair, the empty birdcage in your lap, with the open door, it's exactly like your tattoo! And those prints you used to make!") and also Silas himself, gray-haired but still alive and holding a palette and brush, and again the old man with the kind ice-blue/gray eyes seated in a chair in a blue smock, a woman beside him with one hand on his shoulder, the other clutching an opened crimson parasol, so like the one in Marlise's one photograph of her mother Beatrice ("cochineal" she'd lied to Dr. Lance, so long ago; and where was that photo? Tucked in a book, she thought, so she must have shown that photo to Silas at some point—she must have shown him Bea). And of course the reference to "Paradise"—Silas knew well the name of her family's farm. All those letters from him, so long ago, finding their way to her there. Ah, the letters. Where were they?

Stepping closer, looking harder at the older man in the painting, she recalled the other photograph, the one stuck for years behind the photo she had of her mother. The naked

man with the kindled eyes. Friend of her mother's apparently. This was that man.

"It's uncanny," Elle was murmuring, "the resemblance to you, Mrs. Miles. Truly. Of course, these were familial 'shades,' as he called them, apparently symbolic shadows of who knows what mythic 'origin' figures Silas Newman was conjuring after his shock therapies and his return to his parents' home on the Continent. You can see the flat surfaces, the subtle destabilizing elements of Fairfield Porter's domestic portraits, a bit of Kahlo with the symbolism, don't you think? Still, how surprising."

Miracle, is what Marlise thought, and then she laughed aloud. Maddie glanced at her, worried, but she laughed, too. Even Elle smiled. Then Marlise was crying, and the girls, the young women, were comforting her, leading her back out through the galleries to a proper chair.

They were solicitous and kind; surely they thought, it's because she is Maddie's mother and the city and all the winter walking have tired her. But Marlise felt far from weary. Another missive from Silas! A message to her, lo these many years. Had he imagined her finding this painting one day, decades into the future? He'd had the faith, she marveled, *to imagine her old.* Alive. I see you in all your ages, he had said. Daughter, mother, lover. It was his most eloquent gift, better even than the bristling, talismanic envelopes full of rant and fear and love he'd sent to her when she'd been banished to Paradise Close. This was his offering, generous and visionary. He'd created for her, for himself, for them, a family to come from.

How he had made the painting, where he'd made it, how he'd known about her mother's photo (again, hadn't it been

tucked inside a book? How had he found it? And if he'd found it, where? when?), the umbrella, and whoever the old man was, with the gray and grateful, melancholy eyes—the man from the other photo—of course she wondered.

Somehow none of that mattered. Sitting in the semi-darkness, sipping tap water drawn into a plastic cup by Eleanor from the gallery bathroom, exhaust hum and cinder seeping in from the street, the fragrance of broiled chops and sherry from the restaurants below the High Line, the lacquer odor of the gallery desk, its pile of catalogs, Silas's paintings all around them, Marlise acknowledged and forgave herself at last for her many secrets, and for the way she knew she would continue to keep them. She forgave herself her blind spots, her Leviathan denial, her repression—and also all that she could never discern, all that she had striven and strove to hide or protect. She forgave herself her great good fortune, the luck of living and of having been loved by a precocious, paranoid boy and an ardent poet. And especially the luck of bearing and knowing and loving this beautiful daughter now propping open the gallery door with her sketchbook to let in the fresh cold evening and give her tired, usually reserved, now emotionally overcome mother some air.

And that was the thing about the self, Marlise continued to think (was she actually thinking? Forming thoughts? Silas, Tee, Maddie, perhaps they'd all laugh at her for doubting that she could). The child self, the emerging self, the aging self, any self—is always imperiled. Yet if it is glass-like in its breakability, its fragility, it is also glass-like in its tensility. Its obscurity, its clarity. Both. Its view out, its mirror in. Again, both. Why do some get to live, to survive and thrive, and some do

not? Why are some brought into the light, some blighted by shadow, history, circumstance? Some rescued? Some left behind, forgotten? Why are some saved, and saved and saved again, only to be lost forever? Why are some utterly and for so long lost, only to be graciously, profoundly found?

Silas was not lost, especially not to Marlise, not now. Nor had he lost sight of her. Though time had stopped him, or he'd tried to stop time, even he must have known that a part of each person belongs to the not-Time; it is what is in us before and beyond the whatever that we're born into and expire out of, eluding time's reach. The way Marlise loved that... prism, sky... whatever one wants to call it—in Maddie before she was born, and how Maddie would love and know it in her after she, Marlise, had died. This is how Beatrice and her father must have loved her, Marlise, though they hardly knew one another at all.

And this, of course, was how she'd also loved and continued to love both Silas and Tee despite the ways in which they had been forced to abandon one another. Gathering herself, Marlise recalled something she'd seen framed at the Dickinson exhibit earlier in the day, a fragment—a draft?—Dickinson had written on a scrap of rough wrapping paper. Marlise had copied it out on the back of her program, observing Dickinson's line breaks with slashes. Poems will be letters, letters poems, someone said. Paintings, too, she thought. Paintings will be letters. She recalled the Dickinson passage now, something to do with how we need to read our lives in reverse because trying to understand them forwards is incomprehensible, overwhelming (later, she'd find the exact text as she'd recorded it, "Did you ever / read one of / her Poems back— / ward, because / the plunge from / the

front over— / turned you? / I sometimes / often have / many times have— / A something overtakes the / Mind").

Dickinson had been talking about poems, not life. Whose poems did Dickinson mean, though? Browning maybe. Or Brontë. She'd have to look that up. But, really, what poem? Whose self? Whose story? Her own?

At that very moment, a middle-aged couple who had fallen in love at work were sitting at a table in the juniper-paneled tasting room of the Winery de Paradise Clos in southern New Jersey, raising a glass to their surprised and grateful belief in second chances. As they did so, a blue heron 500 yards away lifted from the splatter-docks along the icy Rancocas. An ancient, three-legged turtle stirred in its muddy winter sleep near an abandoned marina along the brackish shore. Down the creek and across the Delaware, in the last ingot of the day's winter sun over Philadelphia, a young woman who worked as a medical claims adjustor in an insurance office in what once been the psychiatric wing of a progressive adolescent mental hospital, gathered her headscarf against the cold and headed for the parking lot, thinking about how glad she was that it was Friday. In the building that had housed Uncle Fritz's bakery until the early 20th-century, a baby took its first steps across the floor of a subsidized housing loft. Back in Trenton, Zeno Mastrogiovanni, an aged lifer at the New Jersey State Prison, sat in an overheated corner of the cafeteria, his mind ravaged by dementia. On a Virginia lumber road deep in the wilds of Orphan Mountain, the rusted chassis of a car that once crashed, suicidally, into a tree in the midst of a wild autumn storm now bristled with squirrel nests in a shroud of kudzu. Behind a small grocery store, W.C. Caperton and his wife were tinkering among vats of offal in

a refrigerated shed, dreaming of a cure for the cancer that had killed their infant son. In the English basement of a large estate, an aging, lonely man with a gray ponytail and thick glasses sat at the kitchen table and allowed a woman, a very real woman who had forgotten that she once wanted to die, a woman now sitting beside him, to fasten around his wrist a bracelet made of threaded wire and the needle hands and notched face plates of old watches. Throughout the world, the ashes of Silas Newman, long ago dissolved into Lake Geneva, flooded into and out of the luscious, first cause of the cosmos. Back in Manhattan, a graphic artist named Asa, still at her desk, checked her phone to see if her girlfriend had texted to confirm their dinner reservation. And stepping out into the street with Maddie's arm around her, Marlise felt as though she'd emerged from the great, unlooked for charity of reading her own life backwards. A journey that, for one moment, over-turned and overtook time.

Acknowledgments

This brief tale has been long in the making. A little over 35 years ago, I had an inkling for a story I might try to write about a woman who attempts to kill herself in a back-road car crash. She survives, and the amnesia resulting from the wreck keeps her from remembering that she had once wanted to die. Her circumstance—somatic, neurological, psychological, emotional—is freighted with a problematic subtext of danger and denial, but it also suggests a clearing, a chance, a different path forward, a way to live. Why I was haunted by this fictional figure would take me many years to fathom, but as other characters and their stories developed around her, I came closer to articulating the question I'd been leaning into: why do some of us survive travail and some do not? And so my first thanks go to Juke, eidolon survivor, the seed of *Paradise Close.*

A book muddled, parsed, and written over several decades owes a tremendous debt to a host of family members, friends, colleagues, students: thank you for your inspiration, your stories, your support, your acceptance, your forgiveness. This is in many ways a book shaped by other books, and I would be remiss in not expressing my life-long gratitude for the words and example of other writers, the living and the dead. I'm also grateful for the extraordinarily generous pre-publication endorsements of *Paradise Close* by real novelists.

Special thanks to Libby Burton, secret sharer of *Paradise Close* as it tentatively emerged from its closet four or five years

ago. What a gracious force you are in the cosmos. To Robin Cole: thank you for your volant birds. Dinah and Rita: how beautifully you've embodied this text. Allison, Annalee, Meryl, and Jonah: I appreciate your advocation on behalf of this book in the world. To Cassie Mannes Murray and Pine State Publicity: Thank you for helping to give this paperback edition of the novel new life. To hodges adams: thank you for the Ariels.

New Jersey; Philadelphia, Pennsylvania; Vietnam; Virginia: all-too-real gardens with my imaginary toads in them. Apologies for my taking more than a little poetic license with more than a few of the geographical, historical, and meteorological details (there was no East Coast Blizzard of '71).

I cannot adequately thank Karen and Michael Braziller, founders and publishers of Persea Books, for believing in me and my work as it has evolved, lo these many years, from poetry to anthologizing and now this foray into fiction. Your vision and commitment to your authors is a rare and treasured gift.

And finally, to Gabe Fried, my editor of nearly two decades: "...when sudden / Such a Praise began / 'Twas as Space sat singing...." No adequate words for it.

About the Author

LISA RUSS SPAAR is the author of six collections of poetry, most recently *Madrigalia: New & Selected Poems,* and a collection of essays, T*he Hide-and-Seek Muse: Annotations of Contemporary Poetry,* a finalist for the Nona Balakian Award for Excellence in Reviewing from the National Book Critics Circle.

She is the editor of four poetry anthologies, including *More Truly and More Strange: 100 Contemporary Self-Portrait Poems,* and a columnist for *Los Angeles Review of Books.* Spaar is Professor of English at the University of Virginia, where for many years she directed the MFA program in creative writing. She lives in Charlottesville.

PRINCE EDWARD ISLAND

An Illustrated History

DOUGLAS BALDWIN

NIMBUS PUBLISHING

This book is dedicated to my wife, Patty,
my best friend and travelling companion.

Copyright © Douglas Baldwin 2009

All rights reserved. No part of this book may be reproduced, stored in a retrieval system or transmitted in any form or by any means without the prior written permission from the publisher, or, in the case of photocopying or other reprographic copying, permission from Access Copyright, 1 Yonge Street, Suite 1900, Toronto, Ontario M5E 1E5.

Nimbus Publishing Limited
PO Box 9166, Halifax, NS B3K 5M8
(902) 455-4286 www.nimbus.ca
Printed and bound in Canada

Design: Reuben Hall

Library and Archives Canada Cataloguing in Publication

Baldwin, Douglas, 1944-
Prince Edward Island : an illustrated history / Douglas Baldwin.
Includes bibliographical references and index. ISBN 978-1-55109-713-8

1. Prince Edward Island—History. 2. Prince Edward Island- Pictorial works.
I. Title.
FC2611B35 2009 971.7 C2008-907737-7

We acknowledge the financial support of the Government of Canada through the Book Publishing Industry Development Program (BPIDP) and the Canada Council, and of the Province of Nova Scotia through the Department of Tourism, Culture and Heritage for our publishing activities.